IN ONE OF THE ONLY structures in the city of Urv that rivaled the airship towers in height, a young man named Ozymandes stared through the lens of an ornate silver-plated instrument into the darkness of the night sky. He jotted notes in a large, leather-bound book, and then pressed his eye to the lens once again.

As he gazed into the viewer, Ozymandes' heart raced. There was no mistake. Something had changed in the face of the never-changing sky. It was a sign—the first in his lifetime. He pulled back, made a couple more scribbled notes, marking positions carefully.

The lens he gazed through was criss-crossed with markers denoting distances and positions. When he glanced into the viewer for the third time, his face drained of all color, and he had to step back to avoid jostling the viewer and disturbing the fine-tuned adjustments he'd spent hours checking. The object had moved, and not a tiny movement, but a significant movement. An entire hash mark on the graded lens.

He marked this quickly in the book, then, without thinking of what might happen to him for defacing the record, he scrawled a set of figures in the margin of the ledger and performed a quick calculation. With a soft cry, he turned—abandoning his post for the first time in his young life, and fled the Chamber of Stars in search of Myril. The High Priest would know what to do, and if he did not, at least the burden would lift from Ozymandes' shoulders.

ABOUT THE SCATTERED EARTH SERIES:
Three authors.
Three worlds.
Three storylines.
One grand setting.
Read each set, and then keep reading to see how they
ultimately connect
as the Scattered Earths come together again!

AVAILABLE & UPCOMING TALES
OF THE SCATTERED EARTH
The Birth of the Dread Remora—by Aaron Rosenberg
"Crossed Paths"—by Aaron Rosenberg
Resistance Falls—by Steven Savile
The Honor of the Dread Remora—by Aaron Rosenberg

THE SECOND VEIL
A TALE OF THE SCATTERED EARTH

BY DAVID NIALL WILSON

Crossroad Press

CHAPTER ONE

THE MAIN CHAMBER OF THE meeting hall of The High Council of Urv was a stately edifice with towering columns and a decorated, vaulted ceiling. It was centered by a huge oval table of polished stone and ringed with ornate chairs covered in plush upholstery. It was, in fact, a statement, and as Euphrankes Holmynn entered, all he could do was shake his head.

Seated around that table, watching his entrance in solemn silence, an array of gray-haired councilmen waited in frowning silence. Euphrankes had been in the chamber before, and he'd known, more or less, what to expect, but the sheer pomposity of it still made him cringe.

The walls were hung with portraits of still more elders. They dated back to the beginning of The Council. When Euphrankes, as a boy, had asked what there had been before the earliest portrait, he'd been cuffed on the ear and told to keep his silence. He had since come to understand that he'd gotten his answer . . . they didn't know.

The rule for all those summoned to The High Council Chamber was silence. There were words to be spoken, but though they called it a court, there were no deliberations to be made. There were lines on old parchment that spoke with the voice of the law, and policy never deviated. That is why, stepping into the center of the room, where a slightly raised circular stage stood facing the base end of The Council table, seemed like such a waste of time and a display of idiocy. Euphrankes already knew what they would say.

It didn't matter. He'd made his request because it was his nature to make such requests. He'd stood his ground because he knew that he was not the only man on the planet who wished that things might change—that it was possible to prove the limitations and proclamations of law were not inviolate. It didn't even really matter that they would say no, because he knew that—in the end—there would come a time when it didn't matter what they thought, or what they said. If he died in the attempt, he would die knowing in his heart what was, and was not, the truth.

The chamber was only dimly lit by a ring of flickering lanterns. The only bright spot was where he stood, a trick of lenses and mirrors, and he knew this was to make it difficult for him to meet their gaze or study their expressions, while making it simple for them to do the same to him. Euphrankes' father had helped in the most recent redesign of the chamber, and he still had the books of notes explaining the structure, construction, and purpose of each architectural tidbit.

It was, in fact, the influence of his father, Edwin, that allowed Euphrankes to be granted any audience at all. He knew that he was a disappointment to The Council. His father had done great things at their bidding. His inventions and his innovations, as well as many of the technologies behind the existing infrastructure of the city, had made their lives easier. Euphrankes, rather than proving helpful, had done little in his life but cause them a long string of headaches for which the only cure had proven a semi-banishment to a private dome outside the city. He wondered grimly where they might send him next if he angered them sufficiently.

A phlegmy cough broke the silence, and Euphrankes stood as calmly as he could, facing the length of the table. It stretched interminably into the distance, and at the far end, in a dim pool of illumination, High Councilor Cumby sat and gazed back at him. At least, Euphrankes assumed the High Councilor was looking at him. At such a distance he might have been asleep, or facing the opposite way entirely.

"Good morning, Euphrankes," Cumby said. Despite the distance, the acoustics of the chamber amplified the old man's voice so that it seemed the two were standing side by side.

Euphrankes bowed very slightly and kept his expression as devoid of emotion as possible. He didn't believe there was any chance of his request being approved, but he didn't want to give them new reason for their denial before they'd even spoken it.

"It is an honor, as always," Euphrankes said.

"Is it indeed?" Cumby asked. "Well, we shall see. I would like to extend my condolences on the loss of your father. He was a great man. He will be sorely missed in the city, and in these chambers. I pray that his passing was a gentle one."

"It was," Euphrankes said. He was surprised at how close his voice came to breaking as he spoke those words. His father had been a great man in the city, but the man Euphrankes remembered—the brilliant mind that had shown him the magic of metal and gears, steam and pressure, mathematics and theory—had been the rock in his life. His father had kept him busy and sane when he'd wanted to rail against The Council and their rules.

"One of the last things he said to me," Euphrankes added,

trying to be as politic as possible, "was that I should send his regards to this council. I've chosen to carry them personally, and hope that you will forgive the indulgence."

A soft murmur ran about the table at his words. Euphrankes figured they were nodding and patting one another on the back. They'd always believed his father to be their tool—a man who would do as he was bid and give no argument. So unlike his son.

In truth, for every project Edwin Holmynn had completed for The Council, he'd completed a dozen others in the streets, taking care of those in need, and studying ways and means to move beyond the stagnant, dying city he'd called home. When a small outlying branch of the veil-roads had become untenable, it was Edwin who, through judicious use of his influence and several daring trips by air, between veils, had salvaged the complex to which his son had been banished. It was as if he'd glanced into the future and prepared a safe haven against the inevitable.

None of that mattered now. What mattered was that the city was dying, and these old fools didn't care. They would be perfectly content to sit back and watch, their laws fiercely clutched in liver-spotted, blue-veined hands, as the city shrank around them, becoming in the end a mass coffin. None of them had that many years of life left, and an equal number of them cared for the well-being of the inhabitants of Urv living beyond their immediate circle of acquaintance.

"We welcome you," the High Councilor said at last. "We are informed that you have a request, and we are . . . eager . . . to hear what you have in mind. Your family has always served the needs of The Council, and of the city."

Again, Euphrankes gave his small, half bow. Then he stood

to his full six foot four inches and squared his shoulders. He was a big man with a slender, muscular frame tapering to powerful shoulders. His hair was long, and he wore it back over his shoulders in a braid, as his father had before him. He knew that they could hear him if he spoke softly, but he chose to project. He wanted to catch them sleeping and maybe, just maybe jostle them awake long enough to win their support.

"As you know," he said, "the roads between the cities are becoming steadily more treacherous. Flights beyond the First Veil run at regular intervals now, carrying cargo and passengers. Still, they are serving a shrinking world."

There were cleared throats and coughs around the room. Euphrankes held his temper in check, and continued.

"It isn't just the cities. The outlying factories and agricultural collectives are failing. Power sources are limited, and the rituals do not always work to repair what has fallen to age or neglect. It is a troubling time."

"Have you come," a voice piped up from his left, "to lecture us on the history of our world, young man?"

Illana Mirkos, eldest of the women serving on The Council, was a shrill, overbearing woman who had never forgiven Euphrankes' father for turning down her offer of marriage. It would have elevated Euphrankes' family to a level where they might—one day—hold a seat on The Council, but Illana had been twenty years his father's senior, and she was insufferable. She was least likely of all the members of The Council to look favorably upon anything Euphrankes proposed.

"No lady," he said, turning to acknowledge her, but unwilling to be cut off before he'd spoken his peace. "I am here talking about our future, and whether, in fact, there is to be such a future if we do not soon take action to ensure it. The prophets predict another ten years might bring a time when there is no ground travel between cities at all; how long can our cities exist without fuel, or food? Our present fleet of airships cannot bear the brunt of such a catastrophe."

"And you have a solution?" High Councilor Cumby cut in. "I assume by your prattle that this is why you are here. You have some way to prevent the roads from crumbling, or to tie the cities one to the other?"

Euphrankes paused. This was the critical moment. What he proposed was actually not intended to help with the roads. It would not, in fact, make moving supplies from one city to another simpler or cheaper. His vision was more far-reaching than that of The Council, and the moment to show that divergence was upon him.

"I have developed a means," he said, ignoring the question and thus dodging the answer, "to travel beyond the Second Veil. The resources of this planet are finite. We lack the material or facilities to repair or rebuild what has fallen. We must look outward, not inward for a solution. We must look beyond the Second Veil, and I have created a ship that . . ."

Several voices rang out at once. They ranged from high-pitched screeching to angry shouts. High Councilor Cumby glared across the expanse of the table to where Euphrankes stood, letting the tumult grow until the room reverberated with the cacophony, then slammed his hand down on a button embedded in the tabletop. A piercing shriek of sound emanated from amplifying tubes around the room. The vibration of the sound met in the center of the room and swirled, swallowing all the words and screams and protests completely. When Cumby released the button, the room was heavy with silence, and Euphrankes stood, his shoulders shaking with startled anger and outrage.

"You dare?" Cumby said. The old man actually rose from his seat at council, a thing Euphrankes had never witnessed.

"I . . ."

Suddenly whatever it was that amplified Euphrankes' voice died, and though he continued to stutter into the void, only the High Councilor's voice could be heard.

"You dare to come before this council and suggest that, not only are the laws and the prophecies to be ignored, but that the very safety of our planet should be violated? You dare to suggest," the old man paused and seemed to gasp for the breath he needed before plunging on, "that we cause the very type of damage we fear every waking moment of every day?"

Euphrankes took a hesitant step backward, nearly toppling from the speaker's platform. He had been caught completely off guard by this attack. He'd known they would not condone his research, but this?

"Your Honors," he said softly.

No one heard him.

"You will leave this chamber," Cumby roared, his voice gathering strength from some unknown and unsuspected source, "and you will not return. You will cease any research you have begun toward this blasphemy. You will bend your efforts to clearing the roads and repairing the veils, or by all that is holy, I will forget my respect for your father, and I will have you cast out."

The silence, if possible, grew thicker at these words. It was one thing to be banished to an outer sphere, where he was cut off from all normal road traffic in and out of the city. It was quite another to be released from the veil into the outer atmosphere of their world. It was far too thin to sustain life, and it was a punishment not meted out in the forty-two years of Euphrankes' life. It was a sentence of death thinly cloaked in false charity.

He turned. Without another word, features rigid and limbs so stiff he felt each step jolt through his frame as if he pounded his bare feet on concrete, he turned and walked away from The Council table. He stared straight ahead, and when he reached the air lock he stepped inside. Two guards stood beside the door to ensure he did not try to return to the chamber. Euphrankes heard the soft hiss of equalizing pressure. As the doors closed he heard the shriek of the High Councilor's silence reverberating through the room once more. He wondered briefly what they had to argue about, now that his humiliation was complete, but could spare it no concentration. The time for talking was behind him, and he knew what he had to do.

"Sorry, father," he whispered.

Then the outer portal opened, and he stepped into the stale, slightly thinner air of the street and turned toward a series of tall, imposing towers.

The city was a series of low-slung, rectangular buildings stacked neatly, like a child's blocks, one atop the other. A quick glance gave the impression that the city was one big, continuous structure, but it was misleading. There were walls and boundaries within each building. Everything was built in layers, and each of those layers was—in one way or another—sealed off from all others.

Gleaming metal conduits wound up and around the walls, climbed over the roof tops and joined at huge, hydraulically activated valves. The buildings were all closed loops of breathable air, filtered and re-constituted. Near the edge of the veil, generators hummed and hissed as they sucked sustenance from the planet beyond, just enough chemicals and gases and droplets of moisture to sustain the system and prevent them from choking on their own exhaust. It reminded Euphrankes of the machines sometimes used to keep medical patients alive and breathing when their bodies began to fail.

As he walked, he felt the city closing in around him with claustrophobic, breath-stealing power. Ahead were the airship towers. Each served as a dock for one or two ships, magnetic plates holding the great vessels in position just above the First Veil. The locks—seams in the veil surrounded by special vacuum seals on either side—were located beneath each berth.

The *Vector* hovered where he'd left her, and Euphrankes made for the lock leading up to his ship with a purpose. He'd never seen The Council so worked up, and was only glad there had been no time for Myril, the High Priest of The Temple, to get involved. There had been no one cast from the city in a very long time—but if there was one on The Council who would relish the opportunity to bring that age-old punishment back into the mainstream of the cities daily life—it was Myril.

Euphrankes reached the bottom rung of the ladder leading up to his platform, and began to climb. As he made his way up, he glanced over at the one structure in the city of Urv taller than The Council chambers. The Temple of the Veils, while as sealed and impregnable as any other building in Urv, had a gleaming white façade of stone and a massive airlock chamber that had once allowed an entire congregation of worshipers to enter at one time. The clang of those huge doors closing had rung like a great bell as they sealed off the faithful. They had remained closed for nearly a decade, but Euphrankes remembered that sound from his childhood, and he shuddered. It had always sounded to him like the doors of a great tomb closing.

On the platform above, two attendants nodded in recognition. One, a tow-headed boy with a big grin, snapped a quick salute.

Euphrankes took a deep breath, expelled it, and willed his anger and frustration to join the stale, filtered air. He managed a wry grin.

"I'm taking off immediately," he called out. "Give me five."

The boy nodded, and Euphrankes entered the bottom lock, which sealed quickly behind him. When the seal was complete, he climbed up through the membrane-like portal to the upper lock, and waited for it to seal behind him. Then, operating the upper lock manually by means of a wheel, he lowered the pressure inside to match the thin, anemic air of the outer atmosphere, and climbed quickly through. He turned, spun the wheel tight, and mounted the dangling rope ladder to the *Vector*.

Above him, Aria had already opened the outer lock. He smiled. Even though it was much more difficult to catch his breath, the sensation of freedom that stole over him each time he left the lower levels behind buoyed his spirits. He climbed, pacing himself and conserving his breath. He didn't want to become lightheaded. If he fell, the odds were not good that he'd recover enough to climb again, or that Aria could get a lift down to him before he suffocated. He could have worn a suit, but he'd always preferred the risk—and the exhilaration—of facing the air beyond the First Veil on his own terms.

He reached the air lock, pulled himself up the last few feet, and closed the hatch. Immediately, fresh air, purified and drawn from beyond the lower veil by his own pumps, flooded the chamber. A moment later he popped his head up through the main hatch and called out without preamble.

"Cast off and get me away from this place."

He closed the hatch, sealed it carefully, and turned toward the bridge. The *Vector* was a large, sleek craft, the largest of its type ever built. His father had begun construction before his death, and Euphrankes had completed the work, adding a number of improvements to the initial design.

The ship worked on very simple principles. The main structure was surrounded by a thick membrane similar in function to the veils on the planet. These membranes were filled with a gas his father had named "Freethion," which was considerably lighter even than the thin air beyond the First Veil. The lightness was caused, in some arcane manner, by a reaction to gravity itself rather than physical weight. The lift was so powerful, in fact, that it was only through the employment of electromagnetic "anchors" that they were able to prevent the ship from shooting skyward and bursting through the upper veil. The magnets also provided steering, as the surface of the planet was rich with iron.

Euphrankes settled into the pilot's seat as Aria made her way around the bridge releasing each anchor in turn. He watched her, and his mood lightened again. She was a slender woman, tall and lithe, dressed in the loose, comfortable clothing of an engineer. She hadn't accompanied him into the city for a number of reasons, not the least of which was her disdain for any attire The Council or temple would deem "appropriate." Her hair hung in dark rivulets over one shoulder, where she'd tied it in the center with a strip of leather.

The two had been companions for more than a decade, ever since she'd come to him to learn the science of the airships. Her family had been cut off from Urv when one of the roadways began losing pressure. Both ends had been sealed, and the only way left between the two cities was through the veils. She'd been a quick student, and though they'd made several trips to visit her parents in Mancea, each time she'd returned. It was the best business arrangement he'd ever made.

The *Vector* was as different from the Chamber of The High Council as Euphrankes could make it. The crew seats were leather. The benches were wood, but though it was sanded smooth and carefully tooled, it was utilitarian. The metal was polished, but it served a purpose. Nothing was frivolous or wasted.

They could fly the ship with only the two of them, but it was designed for a crew of six on extended trips. They had only a couple of hour's flight to and from Urv, so they'd come alone. Aria crossed the bridge, watching the lines and positioning magnets. They steered by the stars at night, and by landmarks by day. The damaged roads between the cities and outposts were easy to spot, even from a great height, and made navigation a simple matter of connecting the dots. The *Vector* was tuned to their habits and their comfort, and the two were more at home on her bridge than they'd ever been in their laboratory, or the city.

Aria set the course, and turned back to him, coming to stand by his side. The front of the ship was a great, thick window, round and spoked with metal reinforced beams. As they gained speed, leaving the city and The Council behind, she said, "So, I take it things did not go well with The Council."

Euphrankes swatted at her playfully and she darted away, laughing.

"I think," he said, settling back, "that The Council and I have finally parted ways."

"It's about time," she said, returning to lean in and kiss him deeply. "I was afraid you were getting boring."

"That," he said, "is the one thing you never have to worry about."

She settled into his lap, and he held her, enjoying the closeness and the warmth, and staring up and out of the domed glass portal into the distant stars.

CHAPTER TWO

THE OUTPOST APPEARED FIRST AS a bump in the flat, monotonous land ahead. Just to the right, Euphrankes could make out the glowing length of one of the great roads. The *Vector* had no need to follow the old paths, but this particular road had once led to his father's home, now his home. There was a dark stretch down the center they'd passed over an hour back. That length of road marked the break in the veil that had resulted in The Outpost being sealed off from the city. Only the airships traveled between, and no ship other than the *Vector* had reason to make a landing there. Not since Euphrankes had been exiled.

The hypocrisy of The High Council was such that they saw no problem in banishing him to The Outpost and requesting work of him whenever the need presented itself. The banishment was a mostly symbolic gesture, as they were well aware he would not have moved back into the city if they'd paid him to do so. They were also aware he'd take the work when he could get it, because it allowed him to trade for the food, supplies, and equipment he needed to sustain himself and his crew.

Over the years Euphrankes had made improvements that allowed The Outpost to be more self-sustaining. He'd brought his own pumps online for oxygen, and since the place had once been a manufacturing facility, it was equipped with its own well and processing plant for water. When the city handed the place over, that plant had been inoperable, but Euphrankes had gotten it working again, and they'd managed to store a great deal of extra water in one of the huge, old holding tanks.

On top of this, they had created a small agricultural pod and begun growing their own food. Euphrankes was under no illusions. The High Council could tire of him at any moment, and when they did, he intended to be ready to survive.

Their landing tower was wider than most. It had been constructed atop one of the great buildings, anchored to the flat stone of the roof. This gave it more stability, and also allowed work crews easier access to when making repairs or modifications. There was a second ship docked at the tower, the *Tangent*. It was larger than the *Vector*, but only about half of the construction was complete. The *Tangent* was the project Euphrankes had been about to broach to The Council. They would not be pleased to know she was half finished before he bothered to mention her.

Without support from The Council, the point was moot in any case. The *Tangent* would require further a lot of time, equipment, and materials to complete. His crew was too small to maintain the *Vector* and finish the monumental task of bringing the *Tangent* to life, and without a considerable influx of Freethion there was no way she could be made stable.

There were other cities he could approach. It would take a good bit of travel, but he thought that he might reach a few of them before The High Council's latest pronouncements rendered him persona non grata. He hated the delay. It would mean months of lost progress. There was Sparana to the east, and along the west road were Kymenae and Bethes. He had contacts in all of them, and in those he had not visited, his father's name would still be known. There was something to be said for being born to a famous parent.

Aria maneuvered the *Vector* into position beside the *Tangent* expertly. Below, five or six ground crew members scurried about. They didn't really need a ground crew to dock, but when Euphrankes returned, his people liked to acknowledge him. The High Council of Urv might not approve of him, but those he supported, and who assisted him in his work adored him. It was yet another trait, along with his talent for engineering, that he'd inherited from his father.

Euphrankes rose and helped bind the anchors, three to a side. They cranked the steering magnets back in until they clamped onto the outer hull and powered down the consoles. When in flight, the *Vector* drew power from solar panels, aided by a charge developed as the forward rotors spun. It was a very efficient system, recharging itself as they moved through the thin, upper air. The batteries were nearly full, but he didn't like to run them down unnecessarily. He never knew when he might have to take off with little notice, and he liked to be prepared.

A few minutes later they dropped through the airlock and climbed slowly through the veil to the tower below. They were greeted by a pair of young men with dark hair and darker eyes.

"Welcome back, sir," the first called out.

"It's good to be home, Myklos," Euphrankes answered. "Lyones, I hope you have something good in line for dinner? I'm starving."

"I'll see what I can do," the man said, grinning. They all shared duties at The Outpost, but Lyones had proven particularly adept in the kitchen, and as such things do, workloads had adjusted to keep him there.

"Where are the others?" Aria asked.

"Bonymede is in the garage, and Slyphie is calibrating the west pump," Myklos said. "It was working fine, but you know how she gets. She said she heard something 'funny.'"

"Then she probably did," Euphrankes said. "One of these days you're going to ignore her and something will blow up in your face."

Myklos laughed. "Did I say it was good to have you back?"

"I wish I'd returned with better news," Euphrankes said. "I'm afraid we won't be going forward with the *Tangent* any time soon, unless we find some miracle supplier of Freethion, and a way to get back into the good graces of The High Council, we'll have to make some long trips to get everything we'll need."

"And when we do," Aria added, "we'll have to make it look like we're trying to find a way to repair one of the great roads. I wasn't there, but from what Frankes says, the idea of piercing the Second Veil in any form sits poorly on The Council table."

"They haven't got the vision of a child," Lyones growled. He finished adjusting the last of the anchors for the *Vector* and turned toward Euphrankes. "Will we leave soon, then? Should I start gathering supplies?"

"Whoa," Euphrankes said, clapping the younger man on the shoulder. "First, we'll have to do some serious planning. We have some communications channels still open, and we'll need to take advantage of those as soon as possible, before The Council can spread their poison too far. They'll be watching for us to ignore their directive. They'd like nothing better than to put a squad of their goons out here to watch us and force us to do their work for them."

They opened the top hatch in the roof of the building

supporting the tower and descended into the airlock. They sealed the door, pressurized, and exited at the top of a steep stairway leading down.

The Outpost was set up to support a crew of twenty men and women. They had nine in total. In its heyday, the factory had produced machinery for many of the great cities. Pumps, airlocks, anything requiring mechanical parts or machined metal. Metal was the one resource no one lacked. The planet was veined with it, and there was a wide variety available. One type of ore actually served as fuel for the furnaces that drove the super-heated forges.

When the roads had begun to erode and leak, a lot of time, effort, and technology had been thrown at the problem. Euphrankes' father, and then he himself, had contributed significantly to patches; systems of airlocks that repaired bad stretches of road, and then, when the failure of the roads became too much to combat, they'd been among the pioneers of the science of lighter-than-air travel that had helped replace the failing highways. It didn't take a genius to see that it was a battle that could not be won. They simply did not have the resources to recreate the sealed roadways, and those in place were not sustainable. Though it would take lifetimes to fail completely, the system of protections that sustained them was dying.

When Euphrankes had brought this argument before The High Council, he was sent back to The Outpost in exile. Then the road between Urv and The Outpost failed, The Temple proclaimed it a sign from the Gods. Euphrankes proclaimed it a relief. He had no need of the road since he had the *Vector*, and the less accessible his laboratory and his home was to those living and working under the influence of The High Council, the better.

They passed through a second airlock and stepped onto

a high walkway like a metal scaffold overlooking the main laboratory. Euphrankes stopped, leaned on the rail, and stared down into the workspace that represented so much of his life.

They had resurrected one of the old forges, and they had the dies and molds necessary to create pumps and many components of the airlocks used in the cities. When they weren't working on the *Tangent*, or upgrading the *Vector*, they spent their time perfecting and creating products they could trade for the things they needed, and for the technology and machinery they couldn't manufacture themselves. The *Vector* could carry a good cargo, and though Urv would not allow large items to be passed through their airlocks, there were other cities with bigger, more liberal docking facilities. Trade had been good.

They descended slowly.

"It's going to be tough to find buyers now," Euphrankes said. "They know what I'm working on, or what I've been working on. They will alert the outlying cities to watch for particular technologies."

"They can't exist without us," Myklos said. "And you haven't seen what we came up with while you were gone. I think maybe we've upped our value a notch or two."

"The patch?" Euphrankes asked, whirling to his assistant. "It works?"

Myklos grinned.

"Like magic. We have already repaired about a hundred yards of road on this side. We didn't go any farther because we didn't know how your audience would go. If we need to, we can get to Urv by land. It is fast, and strong, maybe stronger than the original veil."

Euphrankes stood very still and thought fast. He'd forgotten that the testing would move ahead while they were gone. He'd focused on The Council, but now? If he'd known the patch would work, he might have used it as a bargaining chip. Then his head cleared.

"That's wonderful!" he said. "We could open the road to Sparana. If we do that, we'll be able to open a more serious trade. They have almost everything we need, including one of the largest, fully functional agricultural pods."

"I want to see!" Aria cried in delight.

They hurried down the rest of the steps to the main floor of the laboratory and out through a long passageway to the main grounds. Unlike Urv, there was no need for airlocks on all the buildings. They were in place, but left open. If something serious went wrong, they could be closed quickly, and if the pressure outside the laboratory and the other complexes dropped too far, too quickly, the buildings would seal themselves automatically. For the moment, The Outpost was one of the safest places on the planet.

They crossed the grounds, which were littered with small garden pods, and came to a huge, arched gateway. The largest airlocks in the compound sealed the entrances to the great roads. When they'd begun to fail, portable locks had been placed between the main locks and the bad stretches in the hope that, eventually, they would be able to open them and repair the damage. That had never happened—the technology just didn't exist . . . except, now maybe it did.

"We used a very thin layer of Imperium," Lyones explained. "We created a membrane and filled it with Freethion. Slyphie calculated the exact energy of the magnetic field, and we put it all in place remotely. When we expanded the membrane and activated the magnets . . ."

"The roadway pressurized," Myklos completed the

sentence. "We ran tests for two hours, before we entered, but it was as clear as any street in Urv. The patch covers about three meters—the rift is only a meter and a half. We've been monitoring steadily for about eight hours now. It's as stable as when it was new."

"And powered by magnetism," Euphrankes said.

He stepped through the airlock and waited as they pressurized it, then stepped through on the other side and walked onto the surface of the road. He turned in a circle, and he started to laugh.

"Gentlemen!" he cried. "Ladies! Pay attention. We have changed the world."

CHAPTER THREE

IN ONE OF THE ONLY structures in the city of Urv that rivaled the airship towers in height, a young man named Ozymandes stared through the lens of an ornate silver-plated instrument into the darkness of the night sky. He jotted notes in a large, leather-bound book, and then pressed his eye to the lens once again.

The viewer was an intricate construct designed around layers of magnifying lenses and a sequence of mirrors. Each needed to be adjusted carefully every evening. It was part of the ritual. Ozymandes was particularly careful with the adjustments, and with the rituals, because he truly loved this part of his duties. In fact, it wasn't his night to gaze at the stars at all—he'd traded with one of the older priests who complained of back problems when forced to stand for extended periods.

As he gazed into the viewer, Ozymandes' heart raced. There was no mistake. Something had changed in the face of the never-changing sky. It was a sign—the first in his lifetime. He pulled back, made a couple more scribbled notes, marking positions carefully.

The lens he gazed through was criss-crossed with markers denoting distances and positions. When he glanced into the viewer for the third time, his face drained of all color, and he had to step back to avoid jostling the viewer and disturbing the fine-tuned adjustments he'd spent hours checking. The object had moved, and not a tiny movement, but a significant movement. An entire hash mark on the graded lens.

He marked this quickly in the book, then, without thinking of what might happen to him for defacing the record, he scrawled a set of figures in the margin of the ledger and performed a quick calculation. With a soft cry, he turned—abandoning his post for the first time in his young life, and fled the Chamber of Stars in search of Myril. The High Priest would know what to do, and if he did not, at least the burden would lift from Ozymandes' shoulders.

He took the stairs three at a time, ignoring the danger of slipping, and gulping in the slightly stale air. They only vented the hallways and stairways once a day. The cleaner, more filtered air was reserved for The Temple, and for the sleeping chambers of the priests. Under normal circumstances it was only a minor annoyance, a dryness in the throat as one climbed, or descended, the stair to the Chamber of Stars. At a dead run, the air rasped in his lungs and chaffed his throat. Before he reached the bottom, he'd begun to feel light-headed, and he hesitated. He leaned heavily against the wall and fought to steady his breathing.

It only took a moment for the immediacy of his mission to wash through him once again, and he worked the crank on the airlock so quickly that it made a loud clang when it hit the stops. The sound reverberated from the walls of the narrow stairwell like the voice of a great gong.

He rushed through and sealed it behind him. Even his urgency couldn't offset years of ritual and careful training. The airlocks had to be set. Lives might depend on it one day, and his standing in the good graces of High Priest Myril was tied to careful compliance and absolute attention to detail.

Ozymandes hurried down the main passageway of The Temple. His footsteps echoed, and he tried to keep them silent. The others would soon start poking their heads out of their cells, or the many small chapels that lined the hall. He didn't have time to be chastised, or to engage any of them in discussion, so when the echoes continued, he broke into an all out run.

When he stumbled through the doorway into the High Priest's antechamber, he was out of breath and coated in sweat. Eldrid, Myril's scribe, glanced up from the parchment he was carefully copying with a start, spattering ink over the document in a fine spray. He gaped at Ozymandes for a second, as if trying to comprehend the sight before him. Then he noticed the ink.

Sputtering angrily, Eldrid rose. He reached for his spectacles, yanking them from his face, and started around the desk.

"What is the meaning . . ."

That is as far as he got. Ozymandes stepped around him quickly, gave the scribe an apologetic shrug, and darted through the doorway to Myril's inner chamber without a word.

Two things met his gaze the moment he stepped through the doorway. Myril sat, slumped back in his great leather chair, and quite alone. That was the first. The second was that the High Priest was fast asleep with his feet propped directly in the center of his great desk.

Ozymandes stood very still, not certain how to proceed. He didn't want to wake the old man suddenly—but his news couldn't wait, and if he didn't act quickly, Eldrid would be on him. He didn't have time for a scuffle, or the shouting match that might ensue.

"Your Eminence?" he said.

He spoke softly, and all his words managed to elicit from Myril was a loud snort, followed by steady snoring.

"Your Eminence!" he called out louder.

This time Myril started. He choked back another snort, sat up straight very quickly, and nearly topped from his chair as his feet slid off the desk. When he recovered and sat up straight, he caught sight of Ozymandes, and glared in open hostility.

"What is the meaning of this?" he cried out. "Eldrid! Eldrid get in here at once and . . ."

"Your Eminence, wait," Ozymandes cried.

He stepped forward and actually laid a hand on the polished surface of the High Priest's desk. Under normal circumstances, he would never have dared, but he knew he had only moments to get the old man's attention.

"I have been on duty in The Chamber of Stars, Eminence," he said in a rush. "There is an anomaly—a sign. Something is coming, and very rapidly. I did not know what to do, so . . ."

"Anomaly?" Myril said. "Anomaly? What kind of anomaly? What are you talking about? What . . ."

"You must come," Ozymandes said. "Please, your Eminence. I would never disturb you without good reason. I have seen a great light approaching the city. I observed it for only a few moments, and it moved an entire mark on the lens grid. There is not much time . . ."

Myril's eyes cleared as he came fully awake. Eldrid burst into the room, but the High Priest stayed him with a quickly raised hand.

"You had better be correct, young man," he said, still glaring at Ozymandes, but with less anger now and more purpose. He turned to Eldrid.

"Rouse the others. Send them to The Chamber of Stars immediately."

Eldrid backed out of the room, nodding in confusion.

"Wait!" Myril called after him. "Before you do anything else, send a runner to High Councilor Cumby. He will need to be notified that something is amiss."

"What shall we tell him?" Eldrid asked.

"Tell him that there's an Urv-Blasted anomaly," Myril bellowed. "Tell him that the stars are aligned for great evil. Tell him that the sky has begun to crumble and fall. I don't care what you tell him—get him to The Chamber of Stars."

Eldrid ducked out of the room without another word. Myril rose and stepped around the desk. He had always been an imposing figure to Ozymandes—a symbol of power. In that moment he looked more like a sleepy, confused old man. His hair waved in gray wisps about his head, and his beard was twisted to one side from where he'd leaned into the chair to nap.

"Well, don't just stand there, young man," the High Priest muttered. "Let's go. I want to see your anomaly before any of the others arrive. We will have to study it, and then, we will have to act."

"What can we do?" Ozymandes asked. He regretted the question almost the second he spoke as Myril's eyes filled with ire.

"How should I know? Do you know how many anomalies have been dealt with by The Temple in my lifetime? I'll tell you, just in case you have fallen behind on your studies and don't know. There have been none. Zero. There is never an anomaly, and duty in The Chamber of Stars has been nothing but a peaceful, quiet hour or two of meditation . . . until now. What can we do? I would suggest we pray as we walk, and hope that something occurs to us before your anomaly crashes through the veils and depressurizes the entire city."

Ozymandes lowered his head and followed meekly as Myril stalked out through his chambers and into the great hall. There were still stragglers waiting to complain about the noise, but seeing Myril, they kept their silence. When the High Priest passed through their ranks, Ozymandes at his heels, they fell in behind.

As they opened the airlock and began to file inside, it occurred to Ozymandes to wonder just how much weight The Chamber of Stars was intended to hold. He hoped fervently that they weren't about to find out, because he had the feeling that they already faced a problem beyond the scope of their knowledge and abilities, and even for the High Priest, one such catastrophe at a time was more than sufficient. Briefly, he wished that he'd gone to his chambers and read a book, rather than swapping for the ill-fated Chamber of Stars duty. Then the airlock opened, and they were climbing the narrow stairs in a long, solemn line, and all other thoughts slowly drained from his mind.

Far away, in the dining hall of The Outpost, Aria happened to glance up through the skylight. She gave a gasp of surprise and rose from here seat, backing so quickly her drink tumbled and spilled across Lyones' lap.

"What?" the big man said, pushing back from the table.

The others had already followed Aria's gaze. In the sky far above, a brilliant flash of light was crossing the skyline.

"That thing is close," Euphrankes said, standing and moving closer to the window where he could see clearly. "Gods . . . it's headed directly for Urv."

"What do you think it is?" Leones asked. "I've never seen anything quite so bright, or close."

"I don't know," Euphrankes said, "but I think we'd better get to work. How many of those patches have you got?"

"A dozen, fifteen maybe," Slyphie cut in. "There will be more by morning. I managed to use some of the old equipment to automate it."

"Before you even knew if it would work?" Aria asked.

Slyphie grinned.

"I always knew it was going to work. It was the rest of you who were skeptical."

Euphrankes laughed, then turned back to gaze at the brilliant chunk of fire dropping from the sky.

"We'd better get going. I think we need to clear the road to Urv, and do it fast. If we can get there with a few of those patches, we might be in time to help."

"Hold on a second," Bonymede cut in. He was a big man, round in the center with slightly bowed legs and arms as thick as most men's thighs. His voice boomed like a loudspeaker. "Didn't they just banish you? Again?"

"That was then," Euphrankes said. "This is entirely different. It's one thing to hold a grudge against the men and women of The High Council—but if that thing causes serious damage to the First Veil in Urv, everyone in the city will be in danger. If we can help, we have to try."

"We could fly in," Aria said. "We'd get there more quickly."

Euphrankes shook his head.

"We couldn't get the equipment in and out of the locks in Urv. We might get them onto the *Vector*, but we'd never be able to unload. The only way in is down the road."

Lyones crossed the room and flipped on a bright light above

a large, square table. He opened a drawer and pulled out a map. It showed the road between The Outpost and Urv. Near the center, on the Urv side, the main breach had been clearly marked. There were several smaller tears marked on either side.

"I think we can drive through," Lyones said, running his finger down the length of the road. "We'll need serious patches here," he poked the map, "and here. These other breaches are small; they won't need a full patch, just an Imperium shield and pressure."

They gathered around and began to plan as the strange, flaming object plummeted closer to the planet, and the High Priests and High Council of Urv met in a mild state of panic, high above the city streets in The Chamber of the Stars. Time was growing short.

CHAPTER FOUR

THERE WERE A NUMBER OF vehicles at The Outpost capable of making the land journey to Urv. Most of them were intended for personnel transport, but in this case, Euphrankes chose the largest in their fleet. It stretched nearly fifty feet in length, and was designed to fit narrowly within the confines of the road, providing maximum cargo space. Before the road had fallen to disrepair, the tracker, as they'd dubbed it, had made regular runs, carrying airlock mechanisms and other products of The Outpost's factories to the city. The return trips had restocked food supplies, and carried in natural resources concentrated in remote areas.

Euphrankes father had discovered the lighter-than-air qualities of Freethion gas, for instance, but had not discovered a plentiful source of it near The Outpost. As it turned out, a large pocket existed on the outskirts of Urv herself, so trade had been brisk. The trade continued, but it was much more difficult to move supplies through the cities' airlocks. The *Vector* could carry quite a bit of freight, but could only deliver smaller items and machined parts to Urv. There was more leeway in some of the other cities, where larger airlocks had been installed and the airship technology had been more fully embraced, but that trade was precarious as The High Council was the acknowledged governing body over all the cities.

Without the roads, though they would never admit it, The High Council and The Temple ruled over a shrinking and dying world. Half the roads out of the city were damaged, and the half that were still in operation were showing signs of wear. The High Council had been forced to change their stance from complete opposition to traveling between the veils to a grudging acceptance. They had taken a stance against progress, and regardless of the stunning short-sightedness of it, the people had followed their lead. Now the entire structure of their society was on the verge of collapsing from entropy.

When the outlying cities had begun work on the Freethion-powered airships, emissaries and priests traveled the roads, usually by foot, to condemn them. When the Merchants Guild approached The Council with plans for the first airship tower, they were turned down, and taxed. It wasn't until the third of the great roads had to be sealed that they acquiesced, and they put strict limits on the size and number of seals that could be attached to the First Veil.

"The veils protect us," Myril had said. "They have always protected us, and to presume to breach that protection is blasphemous and foolish. Each time we allow ourselves to slice another piece of that holy veil, we weaken it—and we show the weakness of our faith. A higher power encased us in the veils and that power can be counted on to protect us in the future—but only if we show faith. Only if we do not presume to know things we were never meant to understand."

The High Council had taken a slightly more lenient, but infinitely greedier stance. They taxed the merchants heavily for anything moving in and out of the city via the airships. They gouged any out-city merchants coming in for trade, and before one could travel from city to city on one of the ships, at least one who was not part of the crew that flew in on it, it was necessary to obtain travel papers and make an insurance "donation" to The Temple.

Euphrankes had not tried very hard to prevent the collapse of the road joining his outpost to Urv. It was the least damaged of the thoroughfares to have been closed off, but he felt safer with the airlocks than he did with The High Council having direct access to his home. If lives had not hung in the balance, he'd never have attempted to reconnect with the city.

Now that they'd committed to re-opening the roadway, they'd split the crew into shifts. Slyphie and Bonymede went in first. Bonymede was adept with the remote-controlled robotic units they used when working beyond the veil, and the first thing they needed to do was to get the patches into place beyond the first seal. Then they could test it by slowly pressurizing that segment of road. If it held, then the next crew, Leones and Myklos, would come in and disassemble the airlock, moving it out of the way and making room for the tracker to pass. They would then perform the same action on the far side of the rift, clearing any debris that might have sifted in from beyond the veil as they passed through.

There was one major leak to get past, and if they were successful, two smaller breaks closer to Urv. The trick would be getting the attention of someone inside the city and convincing them to open the locks. Such a repair was unheard of, believed impossible, and despite the fact that it reinforced the veils put in place by "a higher power," it would no doubt be condemned by The Temple. If there hadn't been a fiery ball of—something— falling from the sky on a collision course with The High Council,

Euphrankes would never have risked it.

While the others worked through the night in shifts, Euphrankes and Aria loaded the tracker and tested its systems. It had been sitting idle for a very long time. They'd even begun using the cargo compartments for extra storage, a practice the pair came to regret before the night was through.

"I wish we had more of the patches ready," he said, driving a small cargo truck up the ramp toward the tracker's hold. Aria controlled the doors and the lifts that moved the cargo into position. The system was designed for the most productivity possible with a small crew.

"We didn't even know if they would work," she said. "And really—what would we have done with them? This is an emergency, and I'll grant you that they may not fine us, banish us again, or throw us in irons, but if we'd taken one of the patches into The High Council, they would have called it blasphemy. They'd say we were meddling with the affairs of higher powers, and the repercussions would ruin us all."

"You're right, of course," he said. "Still, if that thing creates too large of a rift for us to seal, this is all for nothing."

"We'll be running a rescue mission if that happens," Aria said. "I vote we leave The High Council and the priests and cart out women and children first."

"Deal," Euphrankes said with a grin. "That might not be a bad way to fix things, all considered."

He deposited the crate of parts he'd been moving on Aria's lift and backed away.

"It's only going to take about two more trips," he said. "We either have enough, or we don't. I don't want to overload the tracker first time out. I think it's okay—I checked the engines, and the seals are good, in case something goes wrong with the patches and we have to rely on her for life-support, but she's been idle for too long. Machines that are made to move should do so. Otherwise they fall to entropy far too quickly."

"She'll hold up," Aria said. "It seems like a very long time since the roads closed, but it has been less than a year. Things are changing much more rapidly now."

"Thanks to rebels like yourself," he laughed. "It's a good thing we're out here. If it weren't for rogue scientists and rebel engineers, the days of Urv, and all the cities, would be short."

They finished the loading, sealed the tracker, and drove out across the compound on one of the cargo vehicles to check on the road and the seals. The second shift was underway, and they could see, even from a distance, that the patch was holding. Pumps were in place pressurizing the road beyond the portal, and Leones waved to them as they approached.

"I have most of the supports loose," he said. "Once the pressurization is complete, we'll be able to slide them out of the way and move on in. You want to bring the tracker up now?"

"No," Euphrankes said. "Let's give the patches overnight as a test. We can drive the tracker up when we're ready to leave. We're going to try and get some rest. When you finish your shift, do the same. Slyphie and Bonymede will be first up, and they can load food and personal supplies before we hit the road. You two can sleep in the tracker."

"It's been a long time since we did that," Myklos grinned, brushing dust off his hands as he joined them. "I used to love that trip."

"Let's hope we're successful enough that you'll get the chance to make it once or twice more," Aria said. "If we do a good enough job, maybe we can bring the tracker back loaded with Freethion. If we tell them we need it for the patches, we might be able to add enough to the order to finish the outer hull of the *Tangent*."

"Believe me," Euphrankes said, "if we can pull this off, that will be only the start of what I'll be asking for. They'll be able to recreate what we've done on the patches, but not without time to deconstruct one, which they'll have to pay for, and they'll still need someone equipped for the manufacturing. This time, I don't think they have much choice but to deal."

"Progress," Lyones said, "is a road paved with emergencies."

They all laughed. Then, with a few suggestions on how to handle the removal of the debris on the road, Euphrankes and Aria drove back to The Compound and climbed to their quarters. They made their way through the locks and seals quickly, but carefully. With work being done on the road, it was more important than ever that they protect their life-support systems.

"It's going to make me nervous all night," Aria said. "Just the thought of that patch collapsing and all of the air . . ."

"It's going to hold," Euphrankes said. "You know it. You helped design it."

"Old habits die hard," she said. "I'm used to worrying about air."

"With a little luck," Euphrankes said, drawing her after him onto the bed, "We'll soon be dreaming and worrying about space. All around us. Space with no boundaries."

Aria shivered and curled into his arms.

"Sometimes you frighten me," she said.

Euphrankes laughed and kissed her on the cheek. They slept like that, tangled around and over one another, as their world changed around them, shaping their dreams.

CHAPTER FIVE

MAESTER ZINS STOOD ON THE bridge of the airship *Axis*, staring through the great glass windows into the darkness between the veils. They had made good speed, but still he doubted they'd reach Urv before the brilliant object that lit the sky made contact. His men had worked the angles and trajectories, and they believed it would clip the outer shell of the First Veil just on the edge of the city. It could be worse. If they worked quickly, and if the figures were accurate, any rend might be encased by a portal in time not to lose the entire atmosphere of the city.

Zins didn't believe it, though. What he believed was that he and his ship were on a rescue/salvage mission such as the planet had never seen. He'd cut down to a skeleton crew of himself and two others, and emptied his cargo holds. The *Axis* could carry about a hundred passengers in an emergency, and if not laden with other stores. He didn't know how The High Council would determine which hundred would go, but he'd known the minute the fiery object appeared in the sky that he had to act. If he couldn't save them all, he could save some.

The High Council had responded very quickly to his message, asking if they were in need of assistance. Of course, he'd already known the answer to the question, but it was still entertaining to see High Councilor Cumby acting so solicitous. He knew that if the man could have ordered him to come, he'd have done so without hesitation. Zins also knew he'd have to be very careful not to get into a position where The Council could seize his ship.

He had no illusions about The Council's opinion of him. They had condemned air travel, and thus, they had condemned those who pursued it. The fact he was racing to their aid would soften their attitude some, but he needed to be certain he maintained the upper hand in the hours to come.

He had tried in vain to contact Euphrankes Holmynn and the *Vector*. He couldn't believe his old comrade wasn't aware of the threat. Hopefully there was a good reason for his silence, and they'd meet in Urv before all was said and done. It would be a lot easier to maintain his control and to evacuate the city if all the airship captains worked together.

The *Axis* was similar to the *Vector* in function but bore distinctly different lines. Long and sleek with a hull of lightweight Imperium, the *Axis* could maintain higher speeds, but was designed to carry smaller cargo. Maester Zins was a food merchant, and though he made stops at three of the major agricultural pods on his trade journeys, what he carried was insignificant compared to the machinery and technology coming in regularly from The Outpost.

It had long been a wonder to Zins how The Council could continue to antagonize Euphrankes, who, along with his father, had supplied most of the new technology patching their dying city together. Now, with disaster dropping on them from the skies, they would need The Outpost's ingenuity more than ever—and it appeared they might be denied it. If Euphrankes was aware of the threat, and had determined to let the city handle its own problems, then a rift had been torn that might never be repaired.

Termac, Zins' engineer, stepped onto the bridge and broke his reverie.

"We've been tracking that object," he said. "The trajectory has not changed, and the speed is constant. In a little more than a day it's going to make contact with the outer edge of the First Veil. At that speed, and with the heat generated in flight, it's going to be a mess."

Zins nodded.

"We should arrive in time, then," he said. "A lot will depend on how much they've figured out on their own, and how organized The Council can make evacuation. I wish there was somewhere close and safe we could ferry the people to, but we're only going to have time to make it out with one load."

Termac stared out into the darkness.

"There's going to be a lot of people left behind," he said. "Maybe you'd better have Reid and Jen check the weapons. I don't like to think about it, but if they try to storm the ship, we'd better be able and ready to fight them off, or we'll be dying right along with them."

Zins had already considered this possibility. He didn't like to believe that the citizens of Urv would lose control so completely, but it was possible. Who knew how they'd handle the news of their own imminent demise? Myril would no doubt harangue them in The Temple with promises of rewards in the next life, while explaining how he and his priests would be needed elsewhere, to help usher others along their path to fulfillment. Of course, the priests would want to be saved. The Council would want the same, though they were among the oldest and closest to natural death of all Urv's inhabitants. It was going to be a disaster.

Zins slapped his hand onto the intercom button and called for Jen. She'd be able to relay his instructions to Reid, and it saved him listening to his Communications Officer's loud, lengthy opinion on the matter. Under normal circumstances, such rants made Zins smile, but this time he didn't think he could stand it.

A moment later Jen stepped onto the bridge. She was the youngest member of their crew, short with blonde hair and all but invaluable. She knew the electronics systems inside and out, and she could chart by the stars better than any save Zins himself. Her father had served on one of the first airships, and she'd been fascinated by them since her birth. Now she was like family—and Zins hated that he was dragging her into what was to come.

"What's up, Skipper?" she asked, grinning at him.

"Don't call me that," he said reflexively.

"Yes Sir," she replied, tossing in a "Skipper" under her breath.

"We're likely to run into some pretty serious confrontations in Urv," he said. "I need you and Reid to check the weapons. Start with the embedded systems, and then see how we're fitted for portable weapons and protective gear. I hope it doesn't come down to a situation where we need it, but it's better to be prepared."

Jen looked troubled.

"I have family in Urv," she said. "So does Reid; his brother and family are there. How do we decide? We can fit maybe a hundred . . ."

Zins cut her off.

"We can't worry about that now," he said. "We have to see what the situation is when we arrive. It's still possible that whatever damage is done to the veils will be reparable. We've added airlocks for the ships; it should be possible to use the same principle on a break in the outer wall."

"Airlocks for the ship are carefully created," Jen said. "They are very thin tears that are sealed before they are opened. It's not the same thing, and you know it. I can predict where that chunk is going to hit, but not how large the hole will be. Even if we tried to be prepared, we'd need an airlock the size of a house to cover the area where the strike will occur, and the odds are whatever we put in place would be damaged in the collision. This is an evacuation mission, and we'd better get used to it."

Jen didn't wait for a response. She turned and left the bridge, going in search of Reid.

"She's right, you know," Termac said. "There's no way that hole is getting repaired."

"I know that it sounds like a long shot," Zins said, "but I'm hanging onto it because it keeps me sane. I'm not ready to write off a whole city full of people until they're actually gone."

"All the same," Termac replied, "If you have any relatives in Urv, now would be a good time to figure out how you're going to slip them on board. With The Council and the priests, we'll have what—fifty seats left?"

"Maybe we should consider whose stubborn ignorance brought us to this position," Zins said softly. "Without including the priests, or The Council, we could save a lot more people."

Termac stared at him a moment, and then turned to stare through the portal. He didn't answer, but as he turned away, Zins caught the ghost of a grim smile.

CHAPTER SIX

THERE WAS NO IGNORING THE fact that Urv's hours were numbered. They no longer had the luxury of days. It wouldn't be long before the hours dropped away to minutes. The High Council had stood in the Chamber of Stars with the priests of The Temple and watched all that they'd stood for in their long, bitter lives threaten to crumble away in so much flame.

"It is a punishment," Myril had said. "It has been sent because we allowed the piercing of the First Veil, and did not have enough faith."

High Councilor Cumby had heard those words, and something inside that had been frail and brittle for a very long time, snapped. It made no sense. None of it made sense. Suddenly he saw The Council Chamber, which had always seemed such a safe, timeless place, as the empty shell of stone and steel that it was. The air tasted stale, and the huge airlocks that had represented stability and safety for so long felt like seals on a grave.

Now he sat alone at the huge council table. He'd dispatched the others to find any who were loyal and to begin an evacuation. The city was doomed, but the roads—the few roads still safely within the First Veil—were good. If they moved quickly, and if they were very lucky, they could get most of the people into those roads and manage to seal them off from the other side. Some of those escaping might even make it. Cumby didn't believe it, but it was hope, and when everything else is denied, hope must stand tall and be acknowledged.

Myril had sealed himself off in his temple. He claimed to believe that whoever had set the veils in place would come to their aid. He had wasted a lot of precious air bemoaning the ways they had turned from their faith, and the consequences of those transgressions. The truth was, none of the transgressions would have been necessary if their world weren't dying.

Footsteps echoed in the hall beyond the chamber door. A moment later Amharic, the youngest member of The Council, entered the room. He hurried around the table to where Cumby sat, his eyes wild and his hair, only just beginning to go gray at the temples, sticking out from the sides of his head at crazy angles.

"There is an airship!" he cried, as soon as he was in range. "We believe it is the *Axis*, though we have not been able to establish communications."

"A rescue mission?" Cumby asked. "A single ship? They will be able to do little."

"Have you lost your senses?" Amharic asked. He stepped closer and took High Councilor Cumby by the arm. "We must get onto that ship. We must take control of it. If we lose the city, we must survive. The planet needs leadership."

Cumby laughed, and it was a dry sound, devoid of mirth.

"Is that what you believe?" he asked. "Is that really what all of this brings to your mind, that we should gather our tired old bones and seize one of the very ships that Myril and his priests blame this whole disaster on, just so that we can fly away to a different city, seal ourselves in another building, and tell people we know what's best for them? Is that your plan?"

"The Council has always ruled," Amharic said. "What else is there?"

High Councilor Cumby rose from his seat slowly. He was old, but he had cared for himself well. He often walked the streets of the city, taking in details and pretending that all of it was under control—his control. Now he needed to take another walk. He didn't know if they could get onto the *Axis*. He didn't even know if they should try. He did know he would go to the air towers, and that he would do what was expected of him. He would try to survive, and he would try to see that the rest of The Council survived. There was nothing else left to him.

The streets were alive with motion. Cumby had never seen so much life. It wasn't the way things happened in Urv. If you had work, or a meeting, or you needed to visit someone across the city, you exited your airlock, moved through the streets as quickly as possible, and entered the lock at the other end. People avoided the streets, and they avoided crowds, but today—today they were everywhere.

He walked flanked by four large, silent guards, and for the first time since he'd been appointed to The Council more than forty years earlier, he was very glad that they were there. Questions were called out to him, but he ignored them. He met no one's eye. He had no answers for them, and though there were words they'd expect to hear anyway, he couldn't bring the old lies to his lips. He didn't believe in them any longer, and he didn't believe he could look into the eyes of a man or woman likely to die in the next few hours and feed them platitudes. He was afraid he'd scream at them to run. He was afraid he'd push them toward the old roads, and laugh at them for coming to him—to a tired old man who'd spent too many years in a comfortable chair playing God to be of any use to them—for help.

The grounds near the air tower teemed with people. High Councilor Cumby, accompanied by his guards, and Amharic, pushed their way through the center of the crowd toward the nearest tower. It was the larger of the two, and Cumby could see that the rest of The Council was gathered at the base, surrounded by more of the guards. There was no airship in sight, and Cumby wondered briefly if the *Axis* would even arrive before it was too late.

They'd passed two of the old roads on their way. Each had swarmed with workers, and the roads nearby had been filled with lines of men, women, and children with carts and bags, crates and transports of all types, trying to force their way through into the pressurized tunnels without interfering with the workers installing the great airlocks. It seemed impossible that the work could be completed under such circumstances, but to their credit, the citizens of Urv forged ahead.

Once, Cumby had stopped a particularly large group headed for the air towers and directed them back to the nearest road. He'd been surprised how grateful they were that he spoke, and how quickly they listened to him and hurried off to do as he bid them. They were as conditioned as he was. He wondered if they knew he was only sending them to a slightly less likely death. He wondered if they even cared, or if they just needed someone, or something to believe in.

They reached the rest of The Council, and Cumby called them together for a report.

"We have an open communications channel with the *Axis*," Illana Mirkos told him. Her voice was shrill and reedy, much weaker than it sounded in The Council chamber. "Maester Zins has asked to dock. He is aware of the—the object. He wants to help."

"I'm sure he does," Cumby replied. "Has he mentioned how he plans to help?"

"He has to take us on board," Illana replied. Her eyes narrowed, and her voice, if possible, grew even shriller. "He has to take The Council on board so that we can be moved to another city. He . . ."

"Illana, calm down," Cumby said. "It's time we looked at this realistically. Maester Zins does not have to do anything. We could threaten him, but what then? If he does not dock, and does not take anyone on board, the city will be destroyed. We will be destroyed. It would be rather difficult to banish or sanction him from beyond the grave. I don't believe now is the time to try issuing orders or proclamations. How far out is he?"

"I . . ." Illana fell silent.

"He will be docking in less than an hour," Amharic cut in, turning away from the man operating the radio equipment. "He has been clear that he will not open his airlocks unless there is a plan. He has also been clear that he will not allow any force on board his ship that has reason or means to take control."

"In short," Cumby said, "Maester Zins has been dealing with our Council for too many years now not to understand how we operate, and he doesn't trust us. That is going to make it more difficult to save anyone, because if he won't open his airlocks, no one is going to get on board that airship."

There was a commotion in the crowd, and Cumby turned. Myril and his priests were cutting a swath through the center of those gathered, moving more quickly than Cumby could ever remember seeing them. They had no guards protecting them, but they were dressed in all the finery The Temple had to offer. It was enough. The people could not overcome centuries of conditioning. They parted and the priests came through, Myril in the lead, making their way directly to the base of the air tower and the circled Council members.

It was just then that crowd let out a cry. The *Axis* had drifted into sight, high above the city. It looked like a huge, man-made cloud.

CHAPTER SEVEN

THE TRACKER ROLLED SLOWLY THROUGH the portal and into the road beyond. The patches were holding, and the mechanisms and parts from the removal of the airlocks lay piled to either side, ready if they needed it.

Working through the night had paid off. The road was clear as far as they could see. The veil covering the road shimmered overhead, stretching up well above the tracker's roof and a good ten yards to either side. Larger vehicles could make the transit, but the closer they came to filling the space available, the more danger there was of causing a breach. The tracker was the largest legal transit vehicle to make the trip to The Outpost in Euphrankes' lifetime, and they kept it rolling carefully down the center.

Euphrankes had the first shift at the wheel, and Aria sat beside him. They wore protective clothing—leather jackets and soft leather helmets. There were masks, gloves, boots, and breathing apparatus that they could don if they needed to work in an unsealed area. They kept the protective gear to a minimum while safely sealed inside the tracker.

The helmets came with field glasses built in. Normally these were worn back on the head, but Aria had hers down so she could scan the road ahead. It was unlikely that they would run into any sort of detritus on the way, but it had been a long time since the last trip they'd made, and they couldn't be certain that, in the panic over the breach in the veil, things had not been dropped or left behind. They couldn't afford to break down— there was nothing left at The Outpost with enough power to tow the tracker back, and no one ahead was likely to come to their aid—at least not until they reached Urv and did what they could to avert the coming disaster.

The engines ran smoothly, and after the first hour Euphrankes began to relax. It was going to take about half a day to come within sight of the city—and another two hours after that to reach the portal to the city. It was sealed from the inside, and it was going to be hell getting through that seal if they couldn't find someone on the other side willing to take a chance and open it.

The likelihood was that there wouldn't be anyone in the area. The entrance to the road was located in an area of Urv that was mostly made up of warehouses, businesses, and empty housing units where the seals had begun to go fail. There were fewer people living in the city every year and those who did had migrated to the busier central areas near The Council Chamber and The Temple.

Myklos stuck his head in through the door leading to the larger compartments in the back of the tracker.

"You two want some tea? Leones is brewing it."

"I'll have some," Euphrankes said. "Aria?"

She shook her head and concentrated on the road. Euphrankes turned.

"I need you two to be working on how we're getting into the city if they don't open up. I don't want to watch that thing hit from the far side of an impassable barrier. We want to be the heroes of the moment, not too late to help."

"Got it," Myklos said. "I think we're onto something. When we disassembled those portals last night, we spent some time getting more familiar with the mechanisms. The seal at our end is identical to that in Urv, and I think we've found a way in. Lucky for us, it never occurred to The High Council that anyone might try to break into the city, any more than it did that someone might have a reason to open the seal on their way out."

"Even if there wasn't a flaming chunk of—whatever— falling on their heads from space, it would be a good trick to get The High Council to re-open that particular road," Euphrankes said. "They did banish me, after all. I just hope they want the rest of their roads reopened more than they want to punish me for my impertinence."

Aria snorted.

"Impertinence?"

Euphrankes thought back to the *Tangent*, hovering just above the airship tower at The Outpost, an empty hulk.

"You're right. It's not my impertinence that they despise and fear—it's my dreams. That's why they try so hard, time after time, to take them away from me."

"Good thing you sleep soundly, Skipper," Myklos said. He ducked back out of the room before Euphrankes could spin on him.

"Don't call me Skipper," he said softly.

Aria turned and grinned at him, and then returned her attention to the road.

The road's veil shimmered in the refracted sunlight that speared down through the Second Veil above. They had never been able to get a sample of the material that made up the veil itself to study closely, but they knew some things about it. It shielded everything beneath it from spurious radiation. The levels on the surface of the planet outside the sealed domes and arched covers on the roads would have been lethal. Just the sunlight, harmless inside the veil, would fry a man eventually. The atmosphere of the planet, even with the protection of the Second Veil, which enveloped the sky as far as any had ever seen, and was thought to circle the planet, was too thin. It was a poor insulator. Only with the First Veil in place was survival possible. That was how it had always been, and until now—until the fiery disaster had appeared in the sky to set them straight, The Council, citizens, and temple had believed that the way it was was the way it would always be.

"They must be losing their minds," he said.

Aria turned to him. "Who?"

"The Council—Myril and the priests. I mean, everything they have used in the past to shut me down and push me away has come in doubt in the span of a single day. They have to be aware of what's coming. Myril must have seen it from The Chamber of Stars. I always wondered why it was there—what they were watching for. I know he says that those who have always protect us live in the Heavens, and will come one day to set us free. It's all bunch of crap."

Aria smirked. "First you're banished and now blasphemy?"

"You know what I mean," he said. "That chamber is set up to watch beyond the Second Veil, and I think it was set there for exactly this sort of emergency. Whoever, or whatever created the veils—they did so to protect us, yes, but not so that we could become cattle. Not so that their gifts could fall deeper and deeper into ruin, but so that we would have a chance. I believe we were intended to find ways to move beyond what they left us—and beyond the veils. They would not be proud of us for sitting around and worshipping them as their work crumbled."

"They would be proud of you," Aria said. "They will be. If we manage to repair the First Veil in Urv, they are going to have to listen to you. They will have to realize there is no future here."

"They are old," Euphrankes said. "They haven't that many years left in the city no matter what we do. I only hope this shakes the rest of the city up enough that it won't matter what a tired group of old men and women say."

Aria had turned back to the road.

"Slow down!" she called out. "There is something ahead. On the left."

Euphrankes shook himself back into full wakefulness and dropped his own field glasses into place. He followed the line of Aria's gaze and saw what she'd seen. There was a bulky object along the left side of the road. He brought the tracker to a halt and began to scan the veil around that section of road. There was no sign of damage.

"The atmosphere is steady," Aria said.

The door behind Euphrankes opened, and Leones stepped through.

"What's up, Skipper?" he asked.

"Not sure. You and Myklos suit up and get out there. See what that is along the left wall. We have to figure out where it came from. It shouldn't be here—nothing should—and if it came in through a rift somewhere along the way, we could be looking at a collapse ahead."

"Would have to be a damned efficient collapse," Leones said. "There are no leaks in the atmosphere."

"I know," Euphrankes said. "Just get out there and see what it is."

"You got it."

The door closed again, and a few moments later, they saw Myklos and Leones, walking slowly in protective suits, their masks in place despite the safe atmosphere, moving in on the dark object against the base of the shield.

"I can't quite make it out," Aria said.

"I know," Euphrankes said. "It appears to be oblong, like a box."

The radio crackled, and Lyones' voice filled the tracker's cockpit.

"It's a sealed case, skipper," he said. "It's one of ours, or it looks like one of ours. It's been here a long time."

"We dumped some things on the last run," Aria said. "Just to keep our weight down and our speed up. Remember? We didn't have much air."

Euphrankes remembered. They'd been in the road and on their way back to The Outpost when the veil had first failed. While the team at The Outpost had worked frantically getting an airlock in place large enough to prevent loss of atmosphere, they'd been racing for their lives, hoping that the tracker would remain pressurized, and that they could get through the seal at the far end quickly enough not to allow The Outpost itself to become depressurized.

They'd made it, but barely, and it had taken a full week to get their pumps to push enough useable air that they could walk freely on The Outpost's grounds. It had been a mad, crazy rush, but there was one thing that had stuck with Euphrankes—a thing they didn't speak about—that had remained to haunt him.

Aria glanced over at him, caught his expression, and started to speak. Whatever she was about to say, she bit it back.

They watched as Lyones and Myklos dragged the case closer to the center of the road. It was a six-foot long pressurized case, about three feet in on each shorter edge. The two bent and, in unison, released the pressure from either end of the case.

"Here goes, Skipper," Myklos said. He gripped the lid of the case and flipped it up. Moments later, he and Lyones were stumbling back toward the far side of the road.

"What is it?" Euphrankes asked, fearing the answer. "Tell me what you see?"

"A man," Lyones choked out. "There's a man in there, Skipper—he's in a suit, but . . ."

Euphrankes sank back in his seat in shock.

"No!" Aria cried.

Euphrankes knew they had to keep moving. He couldn't let this prevent them from reaching the city, and it was going to be on him to act.

"Seal it," he said. "Get that thing sealed, and then get it into the back. We'll deal with him, whoever he is, when we reach the city. If we don't hurry, we'll be tucking him in with a lot more dead."

"Who is he?" Lyones asked.

"I don't know," Euphrankes said. "We knew others followed us onto the road that day, but we hoped they all got back to the city before . . . Just get him in here."

Euphrankes removed his helmet. Aria rose and came to him, wrapping her arms around his shoulders.

"We couldn't have helped him," she said. "There was no time. We'd all be out here."

"I know," Euphrankes said. "But . . . in a pressure case? He must have found one that we abandoned—a self-sealing case with just enough air inside—given his suit—for what? A day? Two? There's no way to release the pressure from the inside. He must have thought someone was coming back for him. He was waiting . . . for us."

They stood in silence. Lyones and Myklos, once they got moving, had wasted no time. They were out of sight of the windshield and what seemed only moments later, the warning lights flashed off, indicating the tracker was sealed and ready to roll. Euphrankes didn't wait for the others to come to the bridge. He put the tracker in gear and started forward once again. Aria returned to her seat and flipped her field glasses back into place.

They passed three more bodies on their way back to the city. Each time they stopped. There were always spare cases, and they packed each body in carefully. Whoever these men and women had been, they were no more than dry husks. Their suits had contained them, but there was little inside that could be identified. It was a horrible way to die, and it put their mission on sharp perspective as they came into sight of Urv and approached the portal at the end of the road. If they didn't manage to get into the city and succeed in getting their patch in place, thousands could end up like the four they'd found. They might end that way themselves. They were a long way from The Outpost—even longer if they had to make the journey in reverse.

A short distance of the sealed portal, Euphrankes brought the tracker to a slow stop. They all came forward then, and stood beside him, staring ahead at the gateway to the city of Urv. The airlocks were sealed tightly, but they could see around the edges and through the clear veil of the road, and then that of the city, that people were moving in the distance.

"They are trying to evacuate," Euphrankes said. "No one is heading this way—and there is no reason to expect that they would, since this road is considered to be permanently sealed. We'd better get to work."

"You got it, Skipper," Lyones said. "We'll be through in an hour—two max."

"Let's hope it's one," Euphrankes said. "We took some extra time picking up those bodies. We may not have much left."

They turned then and, sealing the cockpit behind them, stepped through into the large central chamber of the tracker. The tools they'd need were laid out for them, and they suited up quickly and silently. There was no reason to fear the atmosphere in the road—their sensors had cleared it as they approached— but they were taking no chances.

"I'll be out in a few minutes," Euphrankes said. "I don't suppose I can raise anyone, but I want to try and get through to The Council and let them know we are here."

"You think anyone is still there?" Aria asked.

"I don't know. Wherever they are, surely they have some means of communication?"

"You may be giving them too much credit," Bonymede grinned.

He stretched and rubbed his eyes. He and Slyphie had been resting. It meant they'd missed the macabre addition to the cargo, and Euphrankes had seen no reason to tell them just yet. They needed to be concentrated and sharp when they got out to the portal.

Euphrankes stepped back through into the cockpit, and the others stepped into the outer chamber of the airlock and sealed the inner behind them.

Euphrankes heard the radio crackle. Frowning, he stepped

over and turned up the volume.

"This is the airship *Axis*," came a familiar, booming voice. "We will not land until the platform is cleared. Please . . . step back from the platform."

Euphrankes nearly answered the call, and then, as if sensing what was to come, he waited.

"*Axis*," a thin, reedy voice replied. It was Illana of The High Council. "Land immediately. The High Council is standing by to come aboard."

Euphrankes had known Maester Zins, Captain of the *Axis*, for many years. He knew the man was no fool. Zins' response confirmed this.

"I repeat," he said. "Stand clear of the landing platform. No one will be boarding my ship without my prior approval, and I will not dock until the platform is absolutely clear. I will be going silent until you comply."

Euphrankes could imagine The Council's reaction. They were used to being obeyed immediately and without question. They were also likely to be very frightened. It didn't bode well.

He reached out, flicked a knob on his radio, and keyed the mic.

"This is Euphrankes Holmynn, calling the airship *Axis*. Zins, you old bastard, come in."

There was silence for a few moments. Then the radio crackled once, and Zins' voice boomed back.

"Frank? Is that you? Where are you, man? I don't see the *Vector* anywhere. It's bad here—could really use some backup."

"I'm here, but we didn't fly," Euphrankes said. He quickly brought his old friend up to speed on what they'd created— what they hoped to accomplish—and where they were at.

"You think it will work?" Zins asked. "You really repaired the road?"

"We did," Euphrankes said. "We have a very large patch. A lot depends on what that thing does when it hits, but if it's a simple rift in the First Veil, I believe we can contain the damage."

"That is the best news I've heard since we saw that damnable chunk of fiery whatever-it-is heading for the city," Zins said. "Let me secure my position here, and I'll get a crew in to help. Hell, I'll come myself. I just have to make sure the bastards don't steal my ship. You know that's what they'll try to do—to move The High Council into the *Axis* and move on to lord it over some other city."

"My thought exactly," Euphrankes replied. "We've got a way through the airlocks; it's just going to take us a couple of hours. Once we're in, we're headed straight for the impact point. I assume you've calculated it as well?"

"Absolutely," Zins said. "We'll get onto the ground, try to talk some sense into the old fools at the base of the platform, and meet you there. If they don't back off the platform, I'll radio my people to lift off and protect the *Axis* until we either succeed, or . . ."

His words trailed off, and Euphrankes felt no urge to complete his old friend's thought.

"I'll see you in Urv," he said.

He flipped off the radio and headed back through the center of the tracker and out the airlock. As he fitted his helmet in place and sealed the insulated rubber at the seams, he tried not to think of another man in a similar suit, laid out in a pressurized metal box in the cargo hold. When he was out, he took off for the others at a run.

Chapter Eight

In the end, it took just over an hour to release the mechanism sealing off the road to The Outpost from the city of Urv. In all the time they worked on it, two at a time in shifts, none on the city side acknowledged their presence. The crews saw passing groups on their way to open roads, or to the airship towers, but it appeared that the seals also cordoned off sound very effectively. With no reason to glance at the road, no one gave it a second thought. It wasn't a way to safety, just another thing closed to them.

Euphrankes gripped the side of a large chunk of the seal, and Bonymede took the other. They counted to three, lifted, and crab-walked the heavy equipment off to the side.

"I wish there was a way to keep it as a backup," Euphrankes said, fighting for breath. "If we don't manage to seal the city, we may have to make a run back to here. It would be nice if we could be certain of re-sealing it."

"Don't even think that," Aria said. She had stepped into the gap left by the open seal. There had been only the slightest shift in pressure as the road and the city became one for the first time in years. She didn't remove her protective gear, but for the moment, it wasn't really necessary. They were as safe as anyone had ever been in the great cage they called Urv.

They hurriedly pulled aside the last of the portal, stacking the pieces as far out of the road as possible. Lyones and Slyphie roamed ahead a little ways, making certain that nothing had been piled or left in the street since the road had closed. It wasn't likely—the citizens of Urv spent as little time in the streets as possible, and the sort of construction that might leave heavy debris was rare. They still had to check. Once they got into the tracker, they needed to keep moving.

The inside of the portal was surrounded by a wide, semi-circular lot. It was as far into the city as mobilized vehicles were allowed. They came through the roads, they unloaded, and what they carried was transported on mechanically enhanced hand trucks and carts. What Euphrankes was about to attempt would have had him banished through the portals with the garbage, or incinerated. He was going to take the tracker through the city streets, eating up valuable air in the process.

There was no reason the vehicle couldn't pass. In the distant past, there had been no such restrictions. Air then had been more plentiful, and the huge pumps that processed what they breathed, and what pressurized their world, had been newer and stronger. As things shifted, and the seals in the roads failed, The High Council began to set down new rules.

Most of them made sense, and under normal circumstances, Euphrankes wouldn't even consider breaking this one, but a bit of fresh air in the face of losing all of it seemed a small price, and the tracker was going to get them to the point of impact a lot faster than they could reach it on foot.

They climbed back in and rolled into the city. The air tower was down the road to their right. There was a main road that ran the perimeter of the city. It joined the different exits leading off to other cities, and had once been alive with commerce. Now it was like a last barrier between the city and the veil. Very few had a reason to cross it unless they were making their way to the airship towers, or assigned to the crews checking the seals.

It had become a superstition; no one wanted to be any closer to the dead air beyond the veil than they had to. It was better to stay sealed up in the buildings than to risk being too far from fresh air to make it back. Euphrankes knew that, regardless of what happened with the patch, this was going to make it worse. Now they would stand in their windows and doorways and stare into the sky. They would wonder what moment would bring that next chunk of debris. He couldn't blame them. Until now, it hadn't even occurred to them.

Euphrankes wanted to reach out beyond the Second Veil. He wanted to find something else—something better—but despite his dreams he had never considered reversing the process. If there was something out there—a place, or another race, who could help their dying planet . . . what else might there be? If something could break the Second Veil and escape into space, why couldn't something fall in?

And if something could fall in, and if Euphrankes could fly out into space—who might fly in, and would they be friendly when they did, or would they take what they wanted, or needed, and leave? Suddenly the rich metal deposits and the pockets of Freethion gas were harder to take for granted.

"If we get through this," he said to no one in particular, "a lot of things are going to have to change."

Aria glanced over at him, but didn't reply.

"Look!" Leones cried.

Euphrankes slowed the tracker, and they all looked in the direction Lyones pointed. Just to their right was the parking lot surrounding the air towers. There were concentric mobs surrounding the base of the tower. Men and women poured in and out of the area, some rushing off to try and find easier safety in one of the main roads before they were sealed off, and others just arriving, hoping to be among the few who could be carried away in the airship.

There was no way for anyone to get safely down from the ship, and Euphrankes could see that no portal had been opened through the veil.

"Gods," he said. "They aren't going to let Zins out of the ship! We could use his help, and if they try rushing the tower, people are going to get hurt. They can't take his ship without his cooperation, but if too many get on the platform and they try to break the seal, they could cause the same damage we're here to prevent, just trying to escape."

He stopped the tracker and climbed out of his seat.

"What are you doing?" Aria asked.

"I'm going to do what I have always done," he said with a sigh. "I'm going to go and try and talk sense to The Council. We need Zins on this, but if we can't get him, at the very least we need to make sure as few people are hurt as possible. If we save the city, I don't want to spend the next week cleaning up dead bodies beneath the towers."

"They won't listen," Slyphie said. "They have never listened."

"This time, I think they will listen," Euphrankes said. "They aren't locked away in a big empty room, they are out in the open, and the people will hear. They will see what we've already accomplished, reopening the road. They have to listen, or we are all lost. Maybe not today—maybe not in this crisis— but soon, and as surely as if it all ended now."

He slipped out of the cockpit and opened the outer hatch. A moment later, he was gone, and the others watched him make his way across the pavement and into the outer ring of the crowd.

"Keep the motor running," Aria said.

Then they sat, and watched, and waited.

The crowds saw the tracker first. It was probably the only thing that got Euphrankes safely through the first wave of refugees and in near The Council. They were still surrounded by their guards, and though the crowd had begun to press forward, the circle held. The only weapons allowed in Urv were in the hands of The Council guard. It was going to take a deeper level of panic for the citizens to charge the circle, but that was only a matter of time.

Euphrankes walked up to the circle and stopped, and then he called out.

"Cumby! High Councilor Cumby!"

At first there was no response. The guards moved toward him menacingly, but he held his ground, glaring back at them, and waited. Then there was a commotion behind that armed line, and he saw Cumby just beyond the shoulders of the guards.

"Let him in," Cumby cried. "Don't you see who it is? Let him in."

Euphrankes was slightly taken aback, but when the opening appeared in the circle of guards, he stepped through without hesitation.

"Euphrankes!" Cumby cried. "Have you brought the *Vector*? Where did you dock? How . . ."

"We repaired the road," Euphrankes said. He didn't allow Cumby to speak, but plowed ahead. There wasn't time to explain everything. "We have a new process . . . it repairs rifts in the veil. I think we can save the city, but you have to let Maester Zins debark—and you have to back away from his ship. There is no time to discuss this. If we move quickly enough, I believe we can seal whatever tear this—thing—makes in the veil. If we succeed, we can help open all the great roads. You have to help me."

Cumby started to speak. Then he glanced over Euphrankes' shoulder into the mobs beyond, and he nodded.

"I'll do what I can. We can hold the base of the tower. If Maester Zins and his crew can get down here and their people can seal off the ship, I'll do what I can to get them out through the crowd."

"You know the point of impact?" Euphrankes asked.

Cumby nodded. "Of course."

"Get him there. It may not be too late for Urv, but there has never been a bigger need for speed. I'm going to go on head with my people. We will get things into position and seal ourselves against the blast. You should get these people into the other roads, or seal them back into the buildings. "

"I will try," Cumby said. "We all will." He glanced over his shoulder at the frightened, huddled council. "I think it's about time we did something for the city."

Euphrankes had about a thousand comments on the tip of his tongue and managed to hold them all.

He turned, and the guards parted. Moments later he was elbowing his way through the crowd and back to the tracker. When he was inside, he called up to the cockpit.

"Get rolling!"

Aria put the tracker in gear and they rolled slowly away toward the city. There were two hours left until impact. Euphrankes prayed that it would be enough.

CHAPTER NINE

THE TRACKER MADE GOOD TIME around the perimeter of the city. Euphrankes knew he could have shaved off some time by cutting across, but there was less chance of running into any unforeseen obstacle on the outer road, and he could crank the engine up to full capacity. Besides, it gave him some small satisfaction to roar through Urv with the engines wide open. Despite the momentary cooperation of The High Council, he had no illusions. They had spurned him too many times for him to trust them so quickly.

"One quarter mile," Aria said.

She was bent over a screen, carefully marking coordinates on a chart beside her. Euphrankes knew that she had long since pinpointed the point of impact. Aria used engineering diagrams and mathematical problems to avoid anxiety. He'd seen it any number of times; starting with the first week she'd come to train at The Outpost. He was glad to have her at this point. If they set up even a little off target, the city could be sucked free of its entire atmosphere before they could adjust.

The plan was simple. They'd brought all of the Imperium they had, and they'd created a thin, impossibly strong membrane. It was set up so it could be pumped full of Freethion, which would draw it up and taut over the edge of the rift. Magnets were attached around the perimeter and in concentric circles moving toward the center. They were precisely calibrated to counteract the Freethion and prevent the patch from being sucked through the rift into space. It was a modification from the patches they'd used on the road. For one thing, it was at least ten times as large as the biggest they'd tried.

The only problem with the design was the placement. They couldn't put it in place until after impact. They would have very little time to get the placement of the magnets right, and once they released the Freethion into the patch, it had to be perfect. Under more controlled circumstances, they could release some gas and loosen the patch, but there wasn't going to be time, and the amount of pressure differentiation was going to be huge. They had a single chance to succeed.

"I'm going to pull up short," Euphrankes called to the others. "If we get too close, we're going to be in danger from the impact."

When the tracker had stopped, they clambered out quickly. All of them were in full protective gear with their helmets sealed. They unrolled the Imperium patch, but kept way back from the veil. They were nearly finished when voices rang out from the direction of the city.

"It's Zins," Lyones cried out, waving.

"Either High Councilor Cumby was as good as his word," Euphrankes said, "or Zins is stuck here with us, and his ship has been taken. Either way I'm glad to have him here. He's got a lot of experience with airlocks, and though this is different, I'm thinking he may have some insight."

"Termac is with him," Slyphie said, "and about half a dozen others. Some of them appear to be in the uniforms of Council Guardsmen."

"Good," Euphrankes said. "The more, the better. Bring them up to speed as quickly as possible," Euphrankes said. "We have less than fifteen minutes to impact, and we don't want anyone who isn't ready at a moment's notice anywhere near that patch. If they don't seem to be getting it, find them something to do a little farther back."

Maester Zins came up at a trot, giving Euphrankes a mock salute.

"At your service," he said. "We got here as quickly as we could. It didn't take too long to get down off the tower, but convincing that crowd to let us leave without allowing them on board the ship was a different matter."

Lyones and Myklos took off suddenly, running back toward the tracker.

"What are you doing?" Euphrankes called out. "There's no time!"

"The debris," Lyones cried. "We forgot. We have to be able to move it out of the way."

And then they were gone around the corner of the tracker, and it was too late to worry about anything. Brilliance filled the sky. There was a whistling, roaring sound from above, and they spun. The thing plummeting out of the heavens wasn't large, maybe the size of a man, but it was dropping at incredible speed. It still burned, despite the thin atmosphere beyond the veil. Euphrankes had little time to worry over this.

"Back!" he cried. "Get back."

And then it struck. The sound was deafening. The object crashed into the veil, moving so fast it pierced cleanly, and hit the ground with a deafening explosion. The shock from the impact drove them back, and they fought for their balance, diving for the edges of the patch.

Lyones and Myklos reappeared. They were pushing one of the hand trucks before them. It wasn't designed for speed; the wheels were too small and low to the ground. It was meant to slowly transport things too heavy to move by hand. It wobbled and careened wildly, but the two muscled it under control. Euphrankes leaped to his feet and gripped the edge of the patch. The hole in the veil was clean, but it was beginning to spider at the edges, and he felt the pressure of the air being sucked out, forced through that one small exit into the gaping void beyond.

The others regained their footing and helped him lift the patch. They all saw the problem at once. They couldn't get to the veil! The debris, still burning, lay between them and the hole, and there was no way to get the huge patch around one side or the other in time.

Then Lyones and Myklos hurtled in front of them, pushing the hand cart crazily. It had a platform with a beveled edge, and they had it lowered as far to the ground as possible. The front of the cart struck the burning projectile and dug in underneath it. Flames shot up and sparks flew. The flames fed on the richer atmosphere of the city, and the fire sucked back toward the hole in the veil. With a scream, Lyones drove into the rear of the cart, Myklos at his side. At first, nothing happened. Slowly at first, and then at a fast skid the cart, and the burning bit of space debris started moving. In only a moment they had rolled it to the side.

"Now!" Euphrankes cried. The group of them lifted the Imperium patch and raced to the veil. As they placed it over the hole, the pressure of escaping air sucked it flat. Aria slammed her hand down on the valve that released Freethion into the membrane. The reaction of the seal was instantaneous. It snapped tight over the hole and sealed to the veil. The splintering, spidering cracks around the edge of the rift stopped spreading. There was a palpable release of pressure as the leak was patched and the city's pumps began restoring pressure.

They all stood back and waited, but the patch held.

"Hey!" Myklos called out. "A little help!"

They turned and saw that the cart had caught fire, burning along with the space debris. Myklos and Lyones had backed away. The heat was too much now, and if they allowed it to continue burning there would be an entirely new threat to the atmosphere. Open flames were outlawed in Urv for very good reason. They ate oxygen.

Slyphie and Bonymede were already rushing to the tracker, and a moment later the others heard it starting up and backed out of the way. Moments later, the big vehicle pulled up beside the flaming cart, and a nozzle extended from the side. The foam it released doused the flames.

They all stood in silence, watching as steam and smoke rose against the side of the veil, leaving a gray-black stain. Then, very slowly, they walked closer, surrounding what appeared to be a jagged bit of metal.

"What is it?" Zins asked. "Gods, it looks like . . ."

"Part of an airship," Euphrankes said. "But not one like any we've ever seen."

More voices sounded from the direction of the city. A crowd was gathering, and at the front of it, Euphrankes saw the High Priest, Myril, and High Councilor Cumby, being born forward on carts that operated similarly to that they'd just used to save the city.

"We'd better get our victory speech ready," Euphrankes said. "Then we'd better figure out what to say when they try and blame this on us."

Zins laughed. "Sometimes," he said, turning to meet the oncoming crowd, "you scare me."

CHAPTER TEN

IN THE END, THERE WERE no speeches, neither of victory, nor of blame. The patch held. The High Council gathered around it, examining the design and congratulating Euphrankes and his people. There were thanks, and it wasn't even mentioned that they'd roared around the city in the tracker, or opened an ancient road back into Urv without authorization.

They all trekked back to The Council Chamber, where food and drink was served. They passed the citizenry of Urv on their way back to their homes. There were some cheers. Some were still frightened half out of their wits. Euphrankes was impressed with the way the councilors and priests reached out to those they passed and set them at ease. It was a talent that he had never possessed—he was too likely to say exactly what he thought without considering how others might react.

Behind them, the chunk of debris was being cooled. It would follow them to the main Council Chamber in due time, where they would all be able to study it at length. There was no doubt that it was a chunk of technology. There was also no doubt that there was no one among them familiar with just what it might be, or with any idea where it came from.

Myril had tentatively suggested that it must be the work

of their own protectors, the all powerful beings who'd sealed them within the two veils. He was quickly silenced as he saw that all present, including the members of The High Council, were unimpressed with this idea.

"Gods, man," Maester Zins said, "you'd better hope not, eh? If this came from The Protectors . . . who destroyed it?"

It was a sobering thought. If one bit of fiery debris could fall from the sky, then why not more? Who had this technology belonged to, and what happened to them? Was it possible that whatever destroyed the original device, ship, or whatever the debris was part of could be heading to their planet? To Urv itself? What would happen if they did?

"I'd like to point something out," Euphrankes said when there was a moment's silence. "This—thing—fell through our outer atmosphere."

"Obviously," High Councilor Cumby replied. "And?"

"And that atmosphere is still there," Euphrankes said. "Whatever the Second Veil is formed of, it is self-repairing. In fact, it would be pretty naïve of us to believe that nothing has ever dropped from space before . . . it's just that this is the biggest piece we've actually spotted, and it hit the First Veil. Maybe some of the tears in the roads happened this way—we've never explored the damaged areas."

"We can now," Cumby pointed out. "With your patches, we should be able to open all the roads. The other cities need to know what has happened here."

"My god," Maester Zins said suddenly. "We have to tell them about the patches! We have to prepare them in case this happens again."

"I think," Cumby added, "that it's high time we told them a lot of things."

Everyone turned to him then. Euphrankes squared his shoulders and prepared for another face-off.

"Our world is dying," Cumby said. He spoke slowly, thinking carefully before each sentence. "For a very long time now, we have watched as our cities, and our roads closed in on us, and we have done little or nothing to prevent it. The only thing that has kept our society alive is the intervention of the very men and women we've ostracized and persecuted."

He glanced meaningfully at Euphrankes.

"It may not be enough to spread the word," Zins said. "We need to know more about what happened, and we need to know how to protect ourselves, if possible, or how to fight back. It seems to me that all of the years we've been under the 'protection' of whoever built the veils have served more to make us weak than to protect us. We aren't growing—we are dying. Slowly, yes, but surely."

"What do you propose?" Illana cut in. "What can we do other than spread the word and prepare them?"

"We can learn," Zins said simply. "We can expand our knowledge, and reach out for ways to help ourselves, or we can die. The patch is a miraculous thing—it saved the city. Urv will go on—but to what end? If we just continue to watch things crumble, we will die. We have to find out what that thing is that fell from the sky, figure out where it came from and what happened to its source, or we might as well roll over now and pull the veil over us like a shroud."

They were all silent at this.

"We need to go . . . out there," Euphrankes said. "It's what I came here to ask about before. I wanted to pass through the Second Veil. The *Tangent*—the ship I'm building—it's designed for it."

"You're crazy," Myril cut in.

They all turned to him, shocked at the outburst. The High Priest was backing away from them all toward the nearest wall. His hands were up, as if warding against something dangerous, and his eyes were wide.

"All of you—you're crazy," he repeated. "Out there? Out THERE? Where? Where will you go? There is no life beyond the veils. There is nowhere on this planet, or beyond, that you can go. We were placed here by a higher power—we have been protected by the veils. If they are failing—if they are coming apart at their seams—it is just an extension of our own failing faith. We have always stayed within the boundaries—protected the air—followed the laws."

"You are following the laws into oblivion," Euphrankes said. "You are deluded, Myril. If there was anyone out there to protect us, they have either departed, or they are sitting back to see if we waste what we were given, or make something of it. We aren't children, and we need to quit sitting around waiting for someone to take care of our problems for us."

"Blasphemy!" Myril cried shrilly. "It's blasphemy, and I'm not going to listen to it."

He spun then to High Councilor Cumby.

"You have to see what is happening here!" he cried. "You have to stop this! We've been given a sign that we have become lax in our faith, that we have taken too much upon ourselves."

"Listen to yourself, man," High Councilor Cumby said.

Cumby stepped closer to Myril, holding out a hand to try and calm his old friend. Myril kept backing away, but eventually came to rest against the wall with nowhere else to go.

"It's not an easy thing for me to admit that I'm wrong," Cumby said. "We have been holed up in that Council Chamber, and you in your Temple, for so long that nothing else seems to exist. It's easy to believe we know all there is to know, and to squash any opposing opinion.

"But we've been insulated so long, we forgot there was a world out here. When these veils were put in place, they weren't built from the inside. Someone knew we would need the protection, and they gave us a chance. Then they left. Whoever, whatever protected us—that was it. They gave us a chance to survive, and I have to say—looking back over what we've done with that chance, we would be a great disappointment to them if they came back to check on us."

"You are wrong," Myril said. "They will be disappointed now. We are bringing doom down on our own heads just by standing here and talking about this. We have to . . . we have to . . ."

He broke then. Without a word, he turned and dashed from the room, knocking Slyphie aside as he burst out into the hall. Before they could stop him he'd unsealed the main door and was in the street, running for The Temple. His hair was wild, and he nearly fell several times, but moments later he entered The Temple, and the great doors clanged shut and sealed with a soft hiss.

"He'll come around," Cumby said.

No one disagreed with him, or questioned the statement, but they all had their doubts. The Temple was one of the thickest, most impregnable buildings in Urv. The doors locked from within, as did all the sealed portals in the city. It would be next to impossible to get in unless the priests allowed it, and if they all shared Myril's outrage, there was little the rest of Urv could do about it.

"How do we proceed?" Zins asked, breaking the silence.

"What do you need, Euphrankes? What will it take to get the *Tangent* ready—how much have you already done? What can the rest of us do?"

"We have time to plan such things," Cumby said. "Tomorrow. For now, let's see about getting this object in here and seeing what we can learn from it. The city is in a shambles, and we need to calm the people. It's time that we," he waved his arm to encompass himself and the other councilors, "got out there and assessed the situation. We're going to have to organize teams to open the roads. We're going to have to send a team to The Outpost to help continue production on the patches. We will, of course, supply any materials we have access to, including Freethion. To be honest, we've hoarded it so long trying to control the airships that we have quite a supply built up. Storing too much can be problematic, as you know. If our magnets ever failed, we'd be causing our own rifts in the veils."

"I'd be happy to help organize that," Euphrankes said. "If Zins will take Myklos, Leones, and Slyphie back in the *Axis*, they can begin production. The rest of us can follow in the tracker. We can haul back a load of Freethion, and all the Imperium you can spare. It will be a start."

"Done," Cumby said. "For now, we will rest, and we will eat. We can retrieve your tracker tomorrow. I'll arrange to have everything you need made ready."

"I'll be getting back to the *Axis*," Zins said, "and airborne."

Euphrankes stepped forward and held out a hand. Zins shook it.

"Good speed, old friend," Euphrankes said. "When you get there, have them show you the *Tangent*. I could use your help on that as well. We can have her ready in a couple of weeks, but . . . I don't have enough to make the crew. She's big."

Zins grinned. "You've got a bargain," he said. "Don't waste too much time on the road."

They separated then. High Councilor Cumby had Euphrankes and those of his people not flying with the *Axis* taken to quarters where they could rest and freshen up, and he called in his guards.

"I will make a short trip through the streets," he said. "I want the people to know that we are back in control, for the moment. Illana, take someone and try to get in to Myril. Try to talk sense to him. We will share our evening meal here—with our guests—and continue to lay plans."

He was silent for just a moment, and then he added, "I believe we are headed into a new age. This is the first day in decades I've felt truly alive."

CHAPTER ELEVEN

WHEN EUPHRANKES WOKE THE NEXT morning, Myril was still sealed in The Temple. There was more activity than he'd seen any day other than the one just passed, as hand carts were rolled from all over the city toward the street just outside The Council chambers.

The tracker had been brought around, he didn't know whether by his own people, or those of The Council. It was parked directly out front, and cargo was being staged. It wasn't until that moment that he remembered what they had on board—and that he'd not mentioned it to Cumby, or any of the others on The Council. He sat up groggily and saw that Aria was up ahead of him. She was seated across the room, brushing her hair. Euphrankes watched for a moment, smiling.

Too often they worked long shifts and crashed, only to get up and do it all over again. It was nice to see her taking time with her hair. She was a very attractive woman, and he felt a sudden burst of pride that she'd linked her life to his own. Then he shook it off and sat up.

"We have to talk to Councilor Cumby," he said.

Aria turned.

"Good morning to you, too," she said.

"Sorry," Euphrankes said. "I saw them down by the tracker, and I remembered what we picked up along the way. We need to take care of the remains. If they have records of those who went missing that day, they may be able to identify them. At the least, they need to receive proper incineration."

Aria stopped combing.

"Gods," she said. "With all that was happening, I forgot about that completely."

"I know," Euphrankes said. "We just got on the good side of The Council—I'd hate to ruin that by having them think we're hoarding dead bodies."

He rose and showered, then dressed as quickly as he could, and the two of them headed out in search of the High Councilor. They found him supervising the work out front, and Euphrankes couldn't help breaking into a grin, despite the grim news he was about to impart. This was the second day in a row he'd seen the High Councilor out of the main chambers, and that was two more times than it had happened previously in his lifetime.

"Good morning," Cumby said as they approached. "I hope you don't mind. Your people were up early, and I took the liberty of having them bring the tracker around so we could get started. I feel as if we need to capitalize on what momentum is available."

"No problem at all," Euphrankes said. "I need to talk with you before we begin the loading, though. We encountered something on the way through the road that you should know about, and it's going to take some special attention. Is Myril still locked down?"

"I'm afraid so. No one has been in or out of The Temple since he sealed it yesterday. Why?"

Euphrankes told him as quickly as he could about the bodies, particularly the man who had climbed into the pressure case to try and save himself. Cumby listened intently, and nodded.

"I'm glad you came to me with this. There are those who are sympathetic to Myril's position, and things are balanced rather delicately at the moment. If they knew of these bodies, they'd find a way to twist it into some sort of sign that we were being punished by the ancients for tampering with the veils."

"But," Aria said, "these people died because the veils failed—not because of anything we did."

"I know that, and you know that, but I'm not sure everyone will believe it, just the same," Cumby said. "As you may be aware," he actually winked at Euphrankes, "we have become a bit set in our ways here. It is much easier to sit back and claim that any action is in violation of the laws of The Protectors than it is to sanction it. They will say that some innovation we made, some change to the old ways, brought about the failure in the road, and that the men caught inside paid the price."

"And yet," Euphrankes added drily, "they have no problem using those innovations to seal off the road and prevent their own punishment. One of the biggest changes and advances was the airlock system."

"I know, I know," Cumby held up his hands. "This isn't the time to get into it, in any case. We need to have those bodies removed quickly and quietly. I'll arrange for some of my private guard to do the work. We can quietly attempt to identify them, notify their families, and perform the proper incineration after you are safely on your way back to The Outpost."

"We appreciate it," Euphrankes said. "I didn't know what to do with them, but I knew I couldn't leave them out there. I would have told you immediately, but, well, we were a little caught up in the moment."

"Indeed," Cumby said. "Tell me, Euphrankes, this ship of yours—the *Tangent*—you really believe it can break through the Second Veil without causing damage?"

"It won't be on fire," Euphrankes said. "From the few tests I've been able to run, and the calculations we've worked out, the Second Veil appears to be less cohesive than the first. While the lower veil is an actual protective, pressurized shell, the Second Veil is apparently solid only to certain types of gas and particulates. I'm not sure how the ancients managed it, but it serves as a sort of sieve, preventing larger bits of space debris—to a point—from striking the lower veil, but radiation and most larger solids pass through relatively unscathed."

"We certainly got a close-up view of how that works," Cumby said. "I wanted to have Myril scan the veil where the object penetrated, but I haven't been able to communicate with him. The stubborn old fool has the only powerful telescope available in the city."

"I can give it a look when I get to The Outpost," Euphrankes said. "We have nothing like the Chamber of Stars is reputed to offer, but our instruments are precise. I have been working on a larger telescope, but it's difficult to grind the lenses without access to the workshops in Bethes. They have no air tower as of yet, and the road has been closed for some time."

"I hope to rectify that soon," Cumby said. "They will be the first city we reach out to, once we have sufficient patches to repair the great road. They have been cut off for too long. I'm comforted by the fact that they have their own agricultural pods, but they have limited supplies of water. You never really see how this world operates like a single great organism until you cut off an organ, or sever an artery. We have food and water, so, of course, Myril told us it was a punishment, and we acted on his word. Eventually we would have made contact through the airships, but it might have been too late. What fools we've been."

"Nothing to be done for that now," Euphrankes said. "If you'll see to the removal of the bodies, we'll get out there and ready the tracker for the cargo. We should be able to load up and be on the road by this evening. Zins should already be docking at The Outpost, so by the time we get there, they could conceivably have enough of the patches completed for the first of the roads. If there aren't too many breaks and rifts, then it doesn't take too long. The road to Bethes will be more difficult, though. The tear is nearly halfway between the cities."

"I've been thinking about that," Cumby said. "The work is going to take time. We'll need to send out teams, and they'll have to be in protective gear until the rift is completely repaired. It will be dangerous."

"I'm sure you'll get plenty of volunteers when word gets out that people's loved ones in Bethes can be reached," Aria said. "Some will have family there."

"I had thought of that," Cumby said, "and I also have an idea I want to run past you before you go, Euphrankes. It came to me yesterday soon after you repaired the veil. I believe I have a notion for a modified shield that might be more mobile . . . using a patch cut to the shape and size of the road, it's perimeter a pocket of Freethion and the inside of that ring magnetized. If the work crews could seal the road up to the point they've reached, it could pressurize behind them. It might speed progress and add a layer of safety."

Euphrankes grinned.

"If you ever get tired of your work with The Council," he

said, "you should join us at The Outpost. That's a brilliant idea. I'll try to start on a prototype on the trip out . . . we should be able to send you something to test on the return trip."

"Perfect," Cumby nodded. "Come and see me before you leave. Hopefully I'll have more to tell you about Myril by then, and we'll have some final details to work out, in any case."

Euphrankes nodded. "We'll see you in a few hours then," he said.

Down by the tracker, he spotted Bonymede directing the stacking of a pallet of Imperium strips. Turning to Aria, he nodded toward their companion.

"We'd better fill him in and help him get this organized before he decides we've abandoned him, or been taken hostage."

Aria laughed as they hurried off together to assist in the loading and stowage of the supplies they were going to need for their return. As they pitched in, Euphrankes was already working out a design for the mobile patch in his head. As busy as it was, and as crazed as the previous couple of days had proven, he thought this might just be the finest day of his long life.

CHAPTER TWELVE

IN HIS PRIVATE CHAMBER NEAR the top of The Temple, Myril paced like a caged animal. He had not eaten since locking himself away, and though he'd allowed a servant to bring in water, he'd barely touched it. He couldn't stop running the events of the past days through his mind, worrying at them from every conceivable angle. It was his responsibility to oversee the spiritual safety of those who looked up to him, but that weight had never felt so important, or so impossible to reconcile as it did in those moments.

He'd seen the fiery death bearing down on them. First he'd seen it through the telescope, and then much closer as it plunged through the veils and slammed into the city street. He'd felt the release of pressure, the sudden, imminent touch of The Protectors, ready to chastise them for their lack of faith. That touch, and the attending punishment, had been denied.

He wanted to believe that Cumby was right, that they had to stand up for themselves, and it was the only way to survive, but the spiritual welfare of the city was in his hands—possibly that of the entire world. He couldn't just shake that off.

He ran down the transgressions of the past two decades in his mind, the times when the rules had been bent, or changed, so that some reckless new technology could be employed "for the greater good." That period also marked the greatest growth in damage to the roads, the worst erosion of the atmosphere, and the growing disregard of all that he'd been taught to hold sacred. It couldn't be just coincidence. The more they deviated from the path that had been set for them, the worse things got, and he feared if things got much worse than they already were, none of them would survive it.

In fact, they should not have survived this. If the breaking of the veil was a punishment, then their blatant disregard of what should have been inevitable was a blasphemy. If it was a blasphemy it was his responsibility to rectify it.

He strode to the door and slipped out into the hall. A quick glance in either direction showed that he was alone. He turned toward the airlock, and the long stair leading to The Chamber of Stars. He met no one along the way, and when he reached the chamber, despite recent events, he found no one on watch.

It didn't surprise him. He'd refused all visitors since closing The Temple, and he'd provided no direction. He wasn't ready yet to make a statement—didn't even know what he would say when he did. He hoped that the chamber, a place he'd spent countless hours in the past, would provide him the silence and peace he required to find those answers.

He closed and sealed the door. He didn't believe he was in any danger, but he knew that with the chamber sealed properly, other priests would believe the watch was set, and would not interfere. More than just a place to study the heavens, The Chamber of Stars—and the duty they spent there—was meant as a place and a time of meditation. Almost all of The Temple's activities involved the group. They met for prayers. They carried out rituals that had been passed down to them from earlier generations. The Chamber of Stars was their opportunity to commune with the powers that protected them. It was a chance to think about how they had been chosen and protected by the veils.

There were books on the shelves lining the walls. Some were the journals of past priests. Some were transcribed scriptures—holy documents that, while seldom in total agreement, followed a common thread of compliance. They agreed on the point that was central to their faith. They had been chosen, and they had been protected. Anything interfering with that protection was heresy. Anything heretical should be punished, squashed, hidden away or destroyed. It had always been their way, and until the space debris had crashed through the veil, shattering their security, their way had had the backing of The High Council.

Myril walked to the great brass telescope. It was aimed, as always, straight out through the skylight and beyond both veils. There were thousands of stars out there—he'd tried many times to count them, and failed. He'd always wondered what they represented, if there were other worlds, other chambers with men of faith, watching him as he watched them, but too far removed to be aware.

If there was no purpose to it all, he felt a part of him would die. If they had not been protected because there was something special about them—something that needed to be preserved, then why? By whom? The veils weren't like the technology they'd discovered on their own. There were no airlocks to be opened. The great pumps that supplied their air had worked flawlessly for centuries and there was no indication in any of the journals or records that there had ever been a time they'd understood how it worked. It just did. It was the same with the incinerators, and the exhaust tubes.

No sane being would go to the trouble to create something so perfect just because they could. And now it was crumbling. The more they changed things, the more they tried to make it better, the farther they got from the original plan, the closer to oblivion they fell. It would not be long before they shot craft beyond the Second Veil, hoping to find answers to questions they should never even have asked, and doomed the entire planet.

Myril stared into the stars, and as he did, a peace descended, removing his doubt and filling him with the warmth of true purpose. He knew what he had to do. He also knew he could trust no one to help him. If he shared his plan with even a single other man or woman, it would fail. He was the High Priest, and it was his duty to set things right. They would not thank him— but it didn't matter. The priesthood was a thankless life—a gift of one's self to the world. He would make a final gift, and he would make it count.

He closed his eyes and bowed low before the ancient telescope.

"Thank you," he whispered.

Then he turned, opened the airlock, and disappeared into The Temple, moving with a speed and purpose he hadn't known for many years, and willing all others to overlook his passing.

Chapter Thirteen

THE TRACKER WAS PACKED TO capacity with supplies, and all preparations were complete for the return trip. For the first time in recent memory, Euphrankes found himself reluctant to depart the city. He knew there was work to do, and his excitement over the prospect of outfitting the *Tangent* and taking her through the veils was barely contained, but it was oddly pleasant to sit in the city of his birth, with a man so recently his enemy, and break bread. It was one of those moments to be remembered carefully.

"We should be able to make better time on the return journey," he said. "We've already cleared and checked the road on the way in. The cargo will slow us a little, but not a lot. It's the most work the tracker has seen in a very long time."

"But not the last," Cumby said. "I'm sure of that. I don't know how we could have been content to let the roads in and out of the city fall, one by one, as we sat back and watched. I'm just thankful that you ignored us and took the initiative to come up with those patches."

"I've made something of a career of ignoring people," Euphrankes said. "I believe that, as well, may be behind us at this point. We all have too much to do to spend much time bickering over it."

"Agreed," Cumby replied. "Once you are on your way, I'll be concentrating on organizing the first party to open one of the other roads. The road to Sparana shows the most immediate promise. The rift is less than a mile from the city, and we should be able to provide more safety and life support than we can on longer trips, like that to Bethes."

"If your design works," Euphrankes said, "it will be something of a moot point."

Cumby laughed. "It's only an idea, coming from me—it won't be a design until you are through with it. That's what I always admired in your father. Ideas have come easy to me throughout a long life, but it's one thing to conceive of a thing, and entirely a different thing to have the ability to bring it to life."

"Discovery is its own reward," Aria said. "Just being there at the moment a thing works for the first time can leave me exhilarated for days."

Euphrankes swallowed the last bit of food on his plate, and washed it down with cool water. He rose slowly, and extended a hand.

"I think it's time we got moving," he said. "The sooner we reach The Outpost and join Zins, the sooner all the rest of these plans can get in motion."

Before Councilor Cumby could respond, there was a commotion in the hallway outside the room where they sat. Cumby rose, as one of his pages entered. The young man looked concerned, and Cumby frowned.

"What is it? What has happened?"

"Nothing has happened, sir," the boy replied. "There is a priest outside. He says he has word of Myril, and that it is urgent."

Cumby glanced at Euphrankes, and then at Aria, who shrugged. They hurried from the room as a group to find a young priest pacing the hallway outside the door. When he saw Cumby, he stopped and turned, eyes wide and expression frantic.

"You have to come!" he cried. "Sir, I would not disturb you, but Myril . . . I believe he may have lost his mind."

"What's your name, son?" Councilor Cumby asked. His voice was calm, and as he spoke, he stepped closer and laid a hand on the young priest's shoulder. "Tell me what has happened, and we'll find a way to deal with it."

"My name," the priest said with an effort, "is Ozymandes. It was I who first saw the . . . object . . . in the sky. I was on my way to evening meditation when I saw Myril, the High Priest, he corrected himself, descend the stairs from The Chamber of Stars. I thought nothing of it at first. I thought that perhaps he'd been checking the skies for more danger, or that he'd only needed a bit of time alone to gather his thoughts. I expected him to turn toward the inner temple—to address the rest of us. Instead, he turned away, and he left The Temple. I didn't know what else to do, so I followed."

"Followed him where?" Cumby asked patiently. "Where did he go, Ozymandes, and why do you think it important enough to come to me?"

"He is in the pump house, sir," Ozymandes said. "When he went in, he was carrying a large pipe. I believe he means to damage the compressors."

Cumby and Euphrankes stared at the young priest, mouths agape.

"Gods," Euphrankes said, "he'll kill us all!"

And then he was running. Behind him he heard Councilor

Cumby calling out to the nearest guards, and he heard footsteps. He assumed Aria was behind him, but he couldn't waste time looking back, and he was afraid if he took his eyes off his goal, he might tumble and injure himself. Euphrankes worked hard every day, but there were few places with fresh enough air to support sprinting, and he was not used to such sudden exertion. He hoped he'd reach the pump rooms before he passed out—before they all passed out, never to awaken again.

Myril stood alone in the central chamber of the great pump room. The hum of equipment shivered through the air around him. The machinery was sealed—they had rituals for its maintenance, but none had any idea where they'd come from. They had been studied, and their principle had been duplicated in smaller, less efficient models, but there was nowhere in all the cities that such large machinery could be manufactured, tooled, or designed. The pumps were able to take the thin, weak air of the planet's atmosphere, combined with the small amounts of exhaust the city created, and the expelled breath of the citizens, and draw the essential elements from it to create breathable air. In short, each and every one of the pumps was a miracle.

There had been attempts over the years to include engineers in the care of the pumps, but Myril, and those who'd come before him, had stood their ground. There was no need of an engineer. What they did to maintain the huge machines was precise, intricate, and detailed. It did not require understanding. It was ritual, and ritual was the domain of the priesthood.

Myril knew what the engineers would do. They'd be perfectly capable of maintaining the machines, but they would be equally incapable of turning off their minds as they worked. They would be analyzing the mechanisms, drawing them when they returned to their workshops, experimenting and trying to recreate, or even improve on what they'd seen. They would, in short, not respect the miracles for their own sake, but would only see them as stepping stones toward some selfish gain— some attempt to prove themselves smarter and more clever than anything that came before.

It was the failing of their people . . . of their city. They had been given every gift they needed. They had food, they had air to breathe, and they had the means to continue—if they stuck to the rituals and the teachings that had kept them safe— to continue as long as their faith held. The failed roads were lessons, but they had not gotten through. The fiery chunk of debris, for all its appearance of alien technology, was a warning. Myril thought it was a warning to the rest of the planet—that Urv had failed. Why else would The Protectors have dropped it on them? They had to have known what would happen—thus it was exactly what was meant to have happened.

What The Protectors had not known was the depth of corruption the city had sunk to. They had not taken into account the airships, and the patches, the seals and the airlocks. Even if the veil had been punctured, and the pressure lost, most of them would have survived one way or another, locked away in the various buildings and traveling about in protective gear until they managed to evacuate.

The interior of the pump room was dark. The only illumination was along the panels where Myril's priests checked the readings daily. There were meters for each pump, gauges and valves. The readings had to be precise, and if they required adjustment, the instructions were meticulous. The valves were moved only in miniscule increments, observed, measured again, and on until everything read exactly as it had read every day since the machines were put into service.

It was comfortable. Knowing that things were the way they had always been, and that they would—or at least could—remain that way forever gave the citizens of Urv peace of mind. It gave them a platform of stability upon which to build their lives. When they met at The Temple on the morning of the tenth day of each month, they listened to the stories. They heard the tale of the veils, and how they had been wrapped around the planet, and the city, and the roads to keep them safe.

No one knew who had built them, or placed them. All they knew was what had been left. Instructions, rituals, and protection. They had been given a way of life that could sustain them into the future, and, just as their scriptures warned, it was not enough. If they did not remain diligent in their faith—if they allowed the rules to be bent, or broken, then all of it could crumble, and their civilization would perish. It was happening all around them, and they went blithely on, ignoring what was right in front of their faces.

Myril strode along the banks of gauges. He reached out and ran his hand over the polished metal. He traced the numbers behind the glass faces. As he passed each control panel, he recited the numbers—the readings that should be on each and every dial. He'd known them by heart for many years. He always carried the scripture—it was required—but if every copy of it were destroyed, he would still know what to do. He would still be able to keep those pumps supplying life to Urv—by faith.

And he could make them stop. He knew every proper adjustment—every step of the ritual. He also knew the warnings. He knew what could cause the most damage, what could ruin the air, or stop it completely. He knew how to complete what the flaming debris had begun, and he knew that it was up to him to do it. There was no other way—his faith was strong, but that of the city had failed.

He pulled his arm back slowly, the metal bar gripped tightly in his hand. Before he could swing it, the doors opened, and two men tumbled through. One he recognized immediately—it was Ozymandes—one of his own. He smiled at the young man. Then the smile died on his lips. The second man was Euphrankes Holmynn—and behind him, blasphemy compounding blasphemy, came his woman. There had not been a woman in the pump room in all the years of its existence.

Myril held his ground and brandished the pipe.

"Stay back!" he screamed. "Don't interfere. This is the only way—the way it is meant to be."

"No, sir," Ozymandes said, stepping forward. "The pumps—the veils—their purpose is to protect, and we serve the veils. You can't . . ."

"I must," Myril said. He turned and began to swing the pipe in a hard, fast arc toward the nearest gauge.

"Stop him!" Euphrankes cried. He dove forward. Behind him, he heard Aria grunt with some effort, but he didn't turn. A moment later, he saw something bright and glittering arc through the air over his head. As the pipe struck the valve a glancing blow, something struck Myril as well, crashing into the side of his head. He tried to swing the pipe again, but it fell from his fingers and he dropped to his knees. Moments later Ozymandes was at his side, pulling him back, and cradling him at the same time.

"Get help!" the boy cried. "We have to get him help."

Euphrankes nodded.

"Aria, go!" he cried.

"What about you?" she asked.

He was staring at the valve. A slow drip of—something—was puddling on the floor beneath it.

"You have to help Myril," he said, moving forward slowly. "I have to fix . . . that."

They all stared, just for a moment, and then Aria was running back toward the door and Euprhankes knelt in front of the ancient technology, his mind whirling. He only hoped he was up to the task.

CHAPTER FOURTEEN

BEADS OF SWEAT BEADED ON Euphrankes' forehead as he stared at the ancient mechanism. The gauge that Myril had struck was leaking. He didn't know exactly what it was leaking, but whatever it was had begun to pool on the floor in front of him. The gauge attached simply enough to a brilliant copper pipe. The pipe, thankfully, was intact, and it appeared that the gauge itself twisted on over the end of that pipe, which was threaded.

Euphrankes whirled. Everyone had departed, except the young priest, Ozymandes.

"The rituals," Euphrankes snapped. "Do they mention what to do in case of a leak, or a drip?"

Ozymandes shook his head. "They are very specific to each task. None of the rituals I have performed address event the possibility of a malfunction."

Euphrankes cursed under his breath, and the young priest frowned at him.

"Are there parts?" Euphrankes asked. "Pieces that have been secreted away, or hoarded? I need two things to make this right. I need another gauge to replace the one that's broken, and you and I have to figure out how to cut off whatever is pressurized in this pipe long enough to replace it."

Ozymandes turned, surveyed the room, and shook his head. He was about to speak, when he stopped cold. Euphrankes would have sworn someone had thrown cold water in the man's face.

A moment later, Ozymandes was running toward the back end of the room. Euphrankes took a last look at the puddle on the floor, and the broken gauge, shrugged, and followed. There was nothing he could do unless they found something to stop that leak.

Ozymandes had stopped in front of a wall of cabinets. They were inset into the wall, so there was no way to tell their depth from where Euphrankes stood. Each was locked, but the priest already had a ring of keys in his hand. He searched through them, as if looking for something unfamiliar, found what he sought, and held the key up triumphantly. He knelt at the last locker on the right hand side of the wall, inserted the key, and pulled the door open wide.

Inside, stacked from the bottom to the top, were sealed metal cases. Ozymandes stared at them, concentrating. Euphrankes stepped up beside him.

"What are they?" he asked.

Ozymandes turned.

"I have no idea," he said. "That's why I'm counting on them being spare parts. This is the locker we have been warned never to open. It is one of the first things an acolyte to The Temple is told. They give you a ring of keys that will open all of these lockers. They tell you what is in each. Some have the rituals in them. Others are empty, and still others just hold day–to-day items like lights, batteries, and warm clothing. This one, though," he patted the open door, "is different. They make a big deal of giving you the key to it—but then they tell you never to open it—on threat of banishment or worse, it is never to be touched."

"Nobody ever opens it?" Euphrankes asked. "There's no list—no inventory so the elders could check and be certain their secret—whatever it is—is safe?"

"It is never opened," Ozymandes repeated, as if just realizing what he'd done. "Never. I don't believe even the High Priest knows what is in here."

"We have the door open, and we still don't know," Euphrankes pointed out.

Startled, Ozymandes reached for the first of the metal cases. He pulled it free, and the two of them knelt together, unfastened the catches, and opened it. Inside was what appeared to be a valve of some kind. Not the part they were after, but encouraging all the same. They resealed it and checked the next box. After a while, they stopped resealing boxes and just stacked them to the side. They found a length of pipe, mechanisms the purpose of Euphrankes could only guess at on such cursory examination, bolts, hasps, and—finally—they found three identical boxes, each with a brand new shiny gauge matching those on the pumps.

Euphrankes grabbed one of the cases and ran back to the leak. It had grown much worse. Where there had been a puddle, there was now a pool of liquid. It appeared to be water, and Euphrankes decided he'd just have to trust his instincts. He couldn't fix this without touching the leak, and he had no protective gloves on him—he'd been ready to climb into the tracker and take off for The Outpost. He realized as he examined the problem more closely that he had bigger troubles. No tools.

"I need a wrench," he said, turning to Ozymandes. "Pliers, something. I have to be able to turn this off of the pipe . . ."

The young priest stared at him blankly. Then, as if a bright light had snapped on in his mind, he spun. On the floor, right beside where Myril had fallen, lay the object that Aria had used to take the man down. Ozymandes ran to it and lifted it in triumph. It was a large, adjustable wrench.

"I'm starting to believe," Euphrankes said, taking the tool and setting to work, "that those protectors you and Myril go on about all the time might actually be looking out for us."

Despite the reprieve of finding the part, he knew they were cutting things close. The atmosphere in the city was thin already. If they didn't manage to get this pump back online, it would become all that much thinner. There was also the chance that, if they did something wrong, they'd cause further damage.

"We have to cut this line off," Euphrankes said.

He turned away from the leak and stared back along the length of the pipe to the pump itself. He followed it, Ozymandes at his heels.

"There is no ritual for this," the young priest said. "Or . . . if there is, it's in one of the books I saw tucked into the back of the forbidden locker."

"Yeah," Euphrankes said, trying not to let his voice grow bitter, "I'm sure that if there are maintenance manuals beyond what you've done to keep these things running, they'd be locked away where no one could see them. God forbid we repair something, or make it work better than it already did. I wonder how many people have come up short of breath because we've ignored some vital part of the upkeep on the pumps in favor of shining them and reading gauges?"

Ozymandes didn't answer. They approached the pump, and Euphrankes concentrated. He saw where each of the separate mechanisms attached in line with the others. There were a set number of gauges for each pump, and a set number of valves closer in. He saw two that were attached to the pipe in question. One, he knew, would shut off the flow to that valve. The other, though, was a different matter altogether. He was afraid if he chose the wrong one, he'd interrupt the flow between all the pumps, and cause some kind of cataclysmic failure. On the other hand, if he was right, not doing anything would have the same result. He just had to figure out which valve was which.

"So tell me, Oz," he said, speaking to the young man as if he were a colleague, and not a priest. "How do we figure this out? All of the pumps have one gauge. All of them have two valves."

"Not all," Ozymandes said. He pointed to the first pump. "That one has a gauge, but only one valve."

Euphrankes studied the pipes, grinned, and turned.

"You're a genius!" he said. "The first pump doesn't require a feed from the previous pump, so there is no reason to be able to shut down that loop. It gets fed by—whatever it's fed by— but not by a pipe from another pump. It has only one of the two valves the others have."

The two hurried over to the first pump and studied the snaking, polished brass pipes. The configuration appeared to be exactly the same on every pump except the first one.

"Truth time," Euphrankes said. "If we're right, we can save the day, and the rituals can begin anew. If we're wrong . . ."

"Then we'll be doing what High Priest Myril tried to do, and everyone will die." Ozymandes said, finishing the sentence. "What are you waiting for?"

Euphrankes glanced at the young man, shook his head and kept smiling. "I'm starting to think there's hope for you yet, Oz," he said.

They returned to the cracked gauge, skirted the puddle on

the floor, and made their way carefully back to the two valves. Euphrankes hesitated just a second, and then he reached out, grabbed the valve corresponding to the single valve on the first pump, and spun it. There was a hiss, deep in the machinery.

They stood very still and listened. The pumps put out a very steady, rhythmic thrum. Since the gauge had been cracked, that rhythm had been uneven. Euphrankes didn't realize he'd know this until he found himself listening for it to right itself. At first, there was no change. Then, just for a moment, there was a burp in the rhythm. He'd heard a similar sound in pumps he'd helped design. It usually meant something that had gotten into a line was being forced out. But were there relief valves? Had opening the system to a leak contaminated it?

The burp repeated, and then, with a soft lurch, the pump wound up and, within a couple of moments, returned to its place in the steady, rumbling voice of the pump room. Euphrankes breathed a long, slow sigh of relief.

"Okay," he said. "Let's get that gauge replaced, and get out of here. I'd suggest, once things settle down a little, that you get whoever takes Myril's place to consider handling things differently. The first thing would be to inventory that cabinet . . . after that, I'd set some people studying the manuals in the back. It's possible that these pumps, while working, aren't working to full capacity. It's also possible that we could build more, if we knew how they worked."

Ozymandes took it all in. He didn't commit, nor did he try spewing, The Temple jargon back at the man who had just saved the city—for the second time in less than a day, but it was obvious he was fighting some serious inner battles. It was also likely he was going over in his mind what he was going to say to his fellow priests to explain what had just taken place.

Euphrankes watched him for a moment, and then picked up the wrench and set to work on the gauge. He wanted to get it off, and get that second valve back to the position they'd found it in, before too much more time passed. The pumps might be working like a well-oiled machine, but they were also very old, and any variation could set off a cascade of faults that would prove disastrous.

As he worked, he saw Ozymandes return to the cabinet and begin slowly and meticulously returning the metal cases. He did not return the case that had held the new gauge. He also pulled free a slender volume, paged through it for a moment, tucked it under his arm, and locked the cabinet carefully. Then he returned to stand quietly as Euphrankes finished.

"What will you do?" Euphrankes asked.

They stood, side by side, listening to the pumps. The reading on the gauge had slowly worked its way up until it rested right where it was supposed to rest—equaling the readings on all the others.

"I will simply tell them the truth," Ozymandes said. "We would all be dead if not for you. This building, and these machines—that is all they are. Machines. They beat like the heart of the city, but they are not eternal. If we don't do something to take control of our lives, and our fates, those lives will be severely limited. If they do not listen, I will remove myself from the priesthood. I think I would like to understand how all of this works, and if I can't learn it here?"

He shrugged, and Euphrankes clapped him on the shoulder.

"I'm starting to think we're all going to be fine," he said. "If you need it, though, I can always find room for a good man at The Outpost."

They left the pump chamber and headed back across to

where Cumby and several others were gathered outside The Council chamber . . . something else had obviously happened while they were busy.

"This," Euphrankes said, as they hurried to join the crowd, "is turning out to be a very long day."

Chapter Fifteen

THE *AXIS* DOCKED WITHOUT A hitch beside the *Vector* on the first airship tower at The Outpost. Slyphie, Lyones, and Myklos were all business, securing the airlocks and descending to the platform, but Zins stood for a long time on his bridge, staring over at the *Tangent*. It was huge. The lines were similar to the smaller ships, but it was obvious that she was more durable than the smaller craft. There were twice the normal number of supports lining the outer hull, and the inner hull, an Imperium membrane similar to those used for the patches, was still visible in areas where construction had yet to be completed.

Termac stepped up beside Zins.

"She's magnificent, I'll grant you that," he said. "Most of the cities don't even have a dock that could accommodate her."

"Euphrankes is crazy," Zins said. "But it doesn't matter. I have to get on board that ship, and I have to find out if it can do what he says it can. There are a lot of things to work out in a very short amount of time. I hope he doesn't take his time on the road from Urv."

"He's as anxious as you are," Termac replied. "More so, I'd think. After all—you admire it, but Euphrankes built it."

"He did indeed," Zins said. "Let's get down below and see

what we can do to help get started on more of those patches. I swear, it's like the secret fell into Euphrankes' lap the second it was needed. I don't give two thoughts to the words of Myril and his priests, as you know, but if I were a religious man, I'd have to say our friend appears to be blessed."

The two gathered their crew and descended to the airship platform, then down to the ground of The Outpost. Lyones was waiting for them with one of the small carts, and they rode on to the main complex in relative silence. Zins was the first to break it.

"This would never be tolerated in Urv," he chuckled. "Riding when we could walk, using up precious air . . ."

"We make more than we waste," Lyones told him. "We have our own pumps, and they're working round the clock . . . we also have a recycling system that retains more of what we breathe than the old one did. It's really pretty simple."

"Perhaps," Zins laughed, "but I'm not an engineer, or an inventor. I leave the creation of amazing things to people like Euphrankes—and then I put them to use. Like the *Axis*. You know his father designed her, yes?"

Lyones nodded. "Euphrankes has talked about it. It was one of the first, wasn't it?"

Zins laughed. "The second, to be exact. The first ship—the *Alexis*—crashed. One of the lessons learned in air travel has been to remain between the veils whenever possible. Flying directly over the surface of the outworld affects changes in the way the ships handle. But you know all of this."

"My father was on the *Alexis*," Lyones said. He kept his eyes forward and drove carefully. "He was the navigator."

"I'm sorry," Zins said. "I didn't know."

"It's fine," Lyones said. "It was a long time ago. It was my desire to follow him—to try and find a way to be certain that what happened on the *Alexis* never happened again—that brought me to The Outpost. When I can, I work on navigational systems. We've made quite a bit of progress."

"I'd be interested in going over that with you while we're here," Termac said. "The *Axis* is not a new ship, and our equipment hasn't been updated as often as it might have been if we'd had more support from The Council."

"If there are really protectors out there," Zins said solemnly, "those days are over. I'd be interested in seeing what you've done as well. Have you used any of it on the *Tangent*?"

"We've used everything on the *Tangent*," Lyones said. He grinned, and his grim mood loosened a bit. "The challenges of propulsion and navigation in space—beyond The Second Veil— are much more complex than slipping between veils. We're not certain that we've got it right yet, but there's a point after which you have to trust your instincts."

"That's a lot of trust," Termac said. He smiled, but it was a thin, humorless expression. "I don't think I'll be trying for one of the slots on that one when it points its nose into space. There's plenty to be done here. In any case, I like to navigate by ground that is clearly beneath me, and a sky that is far above, where it belongs."

Zins turned and glanced over his shoulder, back to where the *Tangent* floated silently above her tower. He didn't say anything, but Termac saw and knew the look in his eye. The *Tangent* would not be suffering for volunteers on her maiden voyage.

They reached the main complex and Lyones parked. They climbed out and made their way inside. It took about twenty minutes for Zins, Termac, and their crew to be shown around the workshops and settled into quarters. The Outpost was designed for many more inhabitants than it presently supported, so there was room for all to be comfortable between shifts.

"We've got enough supplies on the *Axis* to get a start on manufacturing the patches," Zins said. "We won't be able to spare any Freethion, but Euphrankes should be here with that soon enough. I have a load of Imperium, though, that I intended for trade. I was delivering it when we spotted that thing dropping out of the sky. It doesn't look like I'll be making that delivery any time soon, and since it was bound for Bethes, they'll be happy to know that some of it may be used in opening the road back so they can travel to Urv."

"Everything is changing," Termac said. "And very quickly. What we counted on as true yesterday has faded into history, and we don't even know yet what to expect from tomorrow."

Slyphie walked up then, and she shook her head.

"I'm not quite ready to buy it," she said. "When we left, High Councilor Cumby was standing in the middle of a crisis, and it was Euphrankes and the rest of us who handled it for him. He was all smiles and handshakes, ready to re-open the roads and usher in change. I say that will last about one day after everything is stable.

"Even if Cumby is being honest, he isn't the only one on that council. Most of them have occupied their seats for decades. They have become used to living in a certain way, being respected and obeyed without question, and they aren't going to let that all go in a day, not even over something like this. And don't even get me started on Myril and his priests . . . if they'd let us in to study those pumps before the roads broke down, there might not be so much call for engineers to build airlocks and patches."

She turned then, not waiting for any of them to answer, and disappeared into the main work area. Zins turned and glanced at Lyones, who shrugged. Myklos laughed out loud.

"She doesn't believe in . . . repressing. And really, who can argue with what she's saying? If we want things to change, we're going to have to step up, take advantage of this situation, and force their hands. The pumps have been getting weaker in Urv for a very long time. Even when I was young we didn't have to seal every door in every building at night. Now they take it as a matter of course. We could travel back then, too. I visited most of the cities with my father before the roads started failing. Then one trip, he went and I didn't. He's been living in Sparana ever since. I tried to get him to fly out with us on the *Vector* one time—I thought he was going to try and take me out of the crew and tuck me away. He's heard 'the call' you see— works in The Temple there. He believes the airships are a sign of the coming apocalypse."

"Aren't they?" Zins asked. "The cities are crumbling. The protections are fading. Even the veils are showing signs of wear and tear, and though we have found our ways of getting around that, they are only bandages on wounds that will never truly heal. The airships and the technology aren't the cause of the coming apocalypse, but if men like Euphrankes and his father didn't see it coming, the airships wouldn't exist. We've come to a time where it may be too late to patch our world back together . . . and that leaves one answer. Find another. Or build it."

"You think the veils will fall?" Lyones asked.

"I know they will. Everything falls," Zins said. "It's the first lesson I learned when I began flying airships. We spend our lives trying to prevent things from coming apart, wearing out, and falling from the sky. The fact is, there is no cure for it. You go a ways forward, and you can't really get back. We're launching into a brand new world; we don't know if it can protect us, or sustain us, we only know that if we stay in this one, we're like a bunch of rusty gears grinding to a halt. I can't be part of that—never could abide the notion of entropy."

"You sound like Euphrankes' father," Myklos said. "I remember long nights working on the *Vector*, everyone pitching in. He'd just talk. It wasn't like we had conversations . . . he told us what he believed, and what he dreamed. He used to talk to Euphrankes like the rest of us weren't even there—but it didn't seem strange. The two of them could make you believe in anything . . ."

There was silence for a moment then. Myklos was lost in memory, and no one wanted to interrupt him.

"He was a great man," Zins said at last. "I knew him for many years, and I never heard him say a harsh word Whenever his name came up, it was in reference to some new miracle—some invention, or procedure that had changed the lives of others. There isn't a person alive in the city of Urv who has not been touched by the man's work in some way, even if they don't know it, or acknowledge it. It's what's kept Frankes from being in more trouble than he might have been. The members of The Council might not be particularly friendly, or useful, but they remember. All of that power young Slyphie was talking about wouldn't be in their hands if the city hadn't changed, and Edwin Holymnn was responsible for the lion's share of those changes. The difference between father and son is that Edwin was patient, and willing to make all the miracles appear to be the idea of those who wanted the credit, while he himself was content just knowing the truth."

"Patience is not Euphrankes' strong suit," Myklos said. "But he's as brilliant as his father—maybe more so. His vision . . ."

He trailed off, but they all knew what he meant. The *Tangent* was so far beyond anything their world had ever known that there were no words to put it in perspective. It was as if he'd been born of a different age—dropped in among them from a future where things that most would consider beyond even their dreams—were just waiting to be accomplished.

"I don't have his vision," Zins said, "but I share at least one dream." He turned his gaze to the sky. "I want to know what's out beyond that second veil. I want to know what fell out of the sky, and why. I just want . . ."

He trailed off again, but they all understood.

"Let's get some food, and divide the work into shifts," Lyones said. "If we leave Slyphie out there by herself too long she's going to come in swinging an Imperium pipe."

They headed for the kitchen then, Zins handing out orders to his people for the unloading of their cargo, while Myklos and Termac conferred on the workers they had, their skills and abilities, and how best to split the labor. Before much time had passed, the machines were thrumming, gears spinning, and the first shift, worn out from a long day of travel and stress, had dropped off to sleep.

Zins stood outside the complex, staring at the road to Urv, and waiting to grow sleepy.

"Don't take too long, Frankes," he said softly. "It's time for us to get to work."

Chapter Sixteen

When Euphrankes and Ozymandes reached the front steps of The Council building, there was a large gathering waiting for them. High Councilor Cumby stood on the step, flanked by Illana and three other members of The Council. Arranged in a semi-circle around them was a group of priests. They were in full regalia, and as soon as they were close enough to make out faces and expressions, Euphrankes saw that they were in a state of high agitation.

Ozymandes dropped back a little. Euphrankes, in turn, stepped up. He understood the young priest's trepidation. They might have just saved the city, but Ozymandes had been a part of an attack on the High Priest, and he'd committed several acts of outright blasphemy in the eyes of The Temple in very short succession. There was no way to know how this was going to play out.

"Euphrankes," Cumby called out. "I assume your presence means that, once again, things are under control?"

Euphrankes passed the priests and climbed the steps to stand closer to Cumby. Somehow it felt more comfortable.

"There was a broken gauge," he said. "Luckily, Ozymandes," he turned and nodded to his companion, "was able to guide me to a spare. We managed to temporarily shut off pressure to the gauge, replace it, and then restore the pumps to normal operation. As far as we can determine, there has been no permanent damage to the system."

"Blasphemy!" a voice in the back of the group of priests burst out.

High Councilor Cumby winced at the outburst, and then turned to the gathered priests. He lowered his head for a moment, gathered his thoughts, and then began to speak.

"These last few days," he said, "have brought us to demanding times. Things are changing at a pace that our people are, frankly, just not equipped to cope with. Our rituals and our beliefs have kept us safe and happy for years, decades—for more time, in fact, than we have records of or comprehension of. It has made us complacent. I believe that the veils were put in place to protect us. It is what I was taught as a child, and it is what I have taught my own children.

"I no longer believe, however," he raised his eyes and swept them across the gathered priests, "that the veils were intended to make us into weak-kneed children. We have spent so much energy fighting our nature—the desire, and the ability to improve things, to grow and learn.

"I am an old man. When I was young, I could do many things that are beyond me now. I was faster, and I was stronger. I hope I am now wiser, but wisdom alone is not always enough. The city—the pumps—the veils—they are not so different from you and I. They are aging, and, like myself, they are weakening. It's just a very slow process."

"They are our salvation," one of the priests said, stepping forward. "They are not for us to understand—but to be thankful for."

"What kind of caring, intelligent protector," Cumby asked the man, "would put us in a decaying cage to die of entropy? I once knew a man—a great man. He spent long hours telling me things I'm only now beginning to understand."

He turned to Euphrankes and laid a hand on his shoulder.

"That man was your father. He told me that he believed the veils were not just for our protection. He believed they were our challenge. They bought us the time to evolve, and learn, to find ways to survive on our own wits and by our own talents. They were put in place to give us a chance, and we need to embrace that chance, rather than shying away from it in fear."

"The rituals have kept us all alive," the priest said. "The Temple has always guarded the pumps, and performed the rituals."

"I am not suggesting that it should be otherwise," Cumby said. "The pumps need to be maintained, and your order has been performing that service for Urv since time immemorial. I would not presume to change it."

"It is already changed," the man said. "You have imprisoned Myril. That one," he turned and pointed directly at Ozymandes, "has broken his vows, desecrated the pumps, and allowed an outsider access to things that even we are not meant to see."

Euphrankes stepped forward. Cumby looked as though he'd try to silence him, and then thought better of it.

"What Ozymandes showed me," Euphrankes said, "had to have been placed in that cabinet by your order. There has been no other with a key, or access, in all the years of the lives of the eldest in Urv. Somewhere along the line, something has happened to obscure things. You have the key to a locker that holds the schematics and manuals for those pumps. I'll tell you what I think, and then you can do as you see fit.

"I think somewhere along the way someone delved too deeply into the workings of those machines. Someone had those parts, and those books, and went too far, trying to repair something, or change something, and it went wrong. Instead of learning from that mistake, whoever was in charge took the coward's way out. They locked it all away and made it taboo. They hid the only parts you have to keep those pumps creating air into the next generation, and they took any chance you—or any of us—ever have of replicating the technology and improving our lot.

"They did it to protect us—to protect you from making similar errors—but it was wrong. We would not have been given minds to think and the ability to improve ourselves just so there would be a convenient thing to hold over our heads and make us miserable as we watch the mechanisms that should keep our children safe, and alive, crumble slowly to dust. That's not the legacy we want to leave. At least, it's not the legacy that I want to leave."

"What you say makes sense," Ozymandes said, stepping forward. He blushed, and it was obvious he had struggled hard with his own feelings to gain the courage to speak. "I have often wondered why there would be a forbidden place—but a place that every single priest in The Temple had full access to. I thought it was a test of our faith. Now I think it was a safety precaution. Those parts were stacked very carefully, and the manuals—once the cabinet was open—were in plain sight, so it was obvious what they were."

"You have betrayed a sacred trust," the older priest said, stepping forward.

The man's face was angry, and Ozymandes stepped back, just a bit. Then he stood his ground and straightened.

"It is very possible that we are only having this conversation, brother, because I opened that cabinet. It is also possible that it is our own pig-headedness, and yes, I include myself in this, that has brought us to this point in the first place. Do you really believe, Brandin," he stepped closer, looking the older priest in the eye, "that it was the right thing for High Priest Myril to do, smashing at the pumps with a piece of pipe? Did he come to you for council? Did he summon The Council and meditate over this problem?

"It is our sacred duty to protect the pumps. The veils are our responsibility. We are what stands between the city, the people, even The Council, and oblivion. We have taken vows to be those protectors. We did not take vows to destroy what we are set to protect. At least—I did not. Myril set himself above The Protectors."

"He was High Priest," Brandin said. "We are sworn to follow."

"Who will you follow now?" Ozymandes asked?

They all turned then, not to Brandin, or to Ozymandes, or even Euphrankes. The gathered priests turned to High Councilor Cumby, and the question was bright in their eyes. The old man seemed shrunken, as if he'd felt for the first time the great weight of the responsibility resting on his shoulders.

"Ozymandes is too young," he said, "and despite the good that has come of it, I would not replace a High Priest with one who has broken his vows. For whatever reason. It sets a precedent that I do not care for. Brandin, you are too set in your ways. I sense that you would be too much like Myril, and I will not put Urv into hands that might harm her."

"What of Cyril?" Brandin asked. "He is not the oldest of us, but he has been longest in service to The Temple."

A slender, gray haired man stepped forward. He met Cumby's eyes directly.

"What say you, Cyril?" Cumby asked. "Are you ready to lead The Temple into a new future?"

"I have been servicing those pumps," the old priest said, "since I was thirteen years old. I know more about them, I believe, than any standing here. I have studied them when no one watched, and I knew what was in that forbidden cabinet. I have crawled in and around every bit of technology the priesthood controls, and I am not the only one. Had I known of Myril's plan, I would have stopped him—gently."

There were murmurs among the gathered priests. Some nodded their heads and smiled at Cyril's words, others muttered and shifted from foot to foot.

Cyril turned to them. "You are bright, intelligent men," he said. "You are dedicated in ways the average citizen of Urv will never understand. You need to understand that we lead by example. We understand things so that we can protect them. We protect them because we understand better than anyone else."

He turned back to Cumby.

"I will lead, if you will back me," he said. "I will also do what I can to help you with Myril, and hopefully bring him around, in time. One thing only I ask."

"What?" Cumby asked, as shocked and surprised as most of the gathered priests.

"That one," Cyril said, pointing at Ozymandes. "We cannot trust him in The Temple. I believe he is honest, but he is also curious, and there are those who might resent him. I ask that he be removed from Temple service."

"But," Ozymandes said, "The priesthood is all I know . . ."

"That's not entirely true," Euphrankes said. Cyril waved him to silence.

"I am not asking that you leave the priesthood," the old man said. "I believe that Euphrankes is planning a journey—a journey beyond the veils. If there is any place I can imagine where spiritual guidance would be a boon—it is on such a journey. I ask that, as representative of The Temple, you accompany this man when he departs Urv."

They all stood in silence a moment, and then Cumby smiled.

"I believe," he said, "that we have a new High Priest in Urv. It seems, Euphrankes, that you also have a new Chaplain for the *Tangent*. Is this acceptable?"

"Of course," Euphrankes said. "And I'd like to note; this is what comes of asking how things can get stranger."

Then Euphrankes brow furrowed.

"What about the . . . cargo we brought in?" he asked. "In all the excitement, I completely forgot about them."

"I will speak to Cyril about them after you have gone," Cumby said. "Every effort will be made to discover details. I will see that you know as soon as we do. I would ask you to stay for the ceremonies, but under the circumstances, I believe it would be better if you got on the road."

Euphrankes nodded. "I will be interested to know . . ." His words trailed off. "I only wish . . ." Again, he was unable to continue.

"No one can fix all of the problems of Urv single handedly," Cumby said. "You are not responsible. No one is responsible, though there might be a sort of community blame to share. If we'd embraced certain . . . changes . . . sooner . . ."

"Thank you," Euphrankes said. He held out his hand, and Cumby shook it. "We will talk again soon. I believe we have some years to catch up on."

Cumby nodded, but didn't speak. The priests, and everyone else who'd gathered, stared, confused, and impatient.

"Well then," Euphrankes said. "If there are no more emergencies, I suppose we should be on our way."

They all laughed, and then, slowly, they dispersed, Cyril to lead the priests back to The Temple, Cumby to The Council chambers, and Euphrankes to lead Ozymandes off toward the tracker, still loaded and waiting for them.

When they reached the tracker, Aria called out to them.

"About time," she said. "Let's get out of here. I'm not sure I have a third heroic act in me."

"Fine," Euphrankes said. "But you owe me a wrench."

They climbed into the tracker, and moments later it was rolling slowly toward the road leading to The Outpost. For the first time that day, the streets of Urv were silent.

CHAPTER SEVENTEEN

EUPHRANKES MADE GOOD TIME ON the return trip, as he'd expected. The road remained clear, and though they stopped along the way to perform pressure tests and check air samples, they found no sign of deterioration in the patches. There were no incidents, and they made radio contact with The Outpost two hours out, letting the crews working there know to expect their arrival, and the delivery of the awaited supplies and cargo.

"Where have you been, Frankes?" Zins bellowed through the speaker. "We've been ready for that cargo for almost a full day."

"You wouldn't believe me if I told you," Euphrankes said, "but when we get in, we'll have a drink, and I'll tell you anyway. Short version, the city almost got destroyed a second time after you departed, the city has a new High Priest, and we have a Chaplain," he glanced toward Ozymandes, "or maybe a new pump technician. I haven't decided yet."

"I won't pretend to have any idea what you're talking about," Zins said, "but I'll pour those drinks."

They arrived to find the entire crew of the *Axis*, plus Euphrankes' people, gathered before the entrance to the road. There were enough of the small transport vehicles for the crew and cargo of the tracker. Euphrankes pulled up just short of the crowd, and stared at them through the tracker's front viewport.

"This is new," he said. "Usually we have to call three or four times to get someone to pick us up."

"It's not every day heroes arrive at The Outpost," Aria said, smiling at him. "I bet they just couldn't stand the idea of waiting any longer to find out what happened after they left."

"I suppose," Euphrankes said. "Still"

Before they were even out of the tracker, several men and women had opened the cargo bay and begun unloading. Bonymede and Lyones pitched in, a bit confused, but happy for the help. It took a surprisingly short amount of time to unload everything they'd brought, and before they knew it, they were on carts and headed back toward the complex. Euphrankes and Aria rode with Zins, and Termac in a cart driven by Slyphie. The others followed in a second and third cart.

"So," Zins said. "I take it that things didn't go smoothly after we left. Was it the patch? Is there a problem?"

"The patch is fine," Euphrankes said. "Let's just say High Priest Myril had a crisis of faith. He decided that the space debris was meant as a punishment. He tried to sabotage the pumps. We barely got there in time, and if Aria here didn't have good aim, he'd have gotten away with it. He broke a gauge, but I was able to replace it with help from our young priest back there," he nodded toward Ozymandes in the second cart. "He knows more than he thinks he does about pumps. High Councilor Cumby got him out of there—wisely I think—before the cries of blasphemy could get too loud."

"And Myril?" Zins asked, interested.

"He's in custody," Euphrankes said. "Cyril is the new High Priest. It sounds a lot like Myril, I know, but trust me, this old guy has been breaking the rules for a very long time, and he's going to be good for that temple. The times are changing fast. I hope, after helping set it all in motion, we're able to keep up."

"Well, we have some surprises for you in that regard," Zins said. "We've been working steadily since we got here. We expected you yesterday, and when you didn't show, we started working on the *Tangent*."

Euphrankes started.

"What have you done?" he asked.

"Relax," Zins laughed. "For my own part, I spent the time with Slyphie learning everything I could. The others worked on preparing the inner lining so that, once we get the Imperium processed, we can begin work on the outer membrane."

Euphrankes felt the weariness drain from him in an instant. Every time he thought about the *Tangent*, he got excited.

"Did Slyphie explain the propulsion?" he asked. "That's my biggest concern. We've done experiments, using the weaker atmosphere between the veils as a guide, but . . ."

"I have some thoughts," Zins said, "but they can wait. "Let's get this cargo into the work area and arrange a schedule. The patches are our first concern. We need to maintain this new relationship with High Councilor Cumby and the rest of The Council in Urv, and the best way to do that is to get a good supply of the patches back to them so that they can begin opening channels to the other cities. We may not be able to rebuild our world, but I think we have a good shot at repairing it so it can carry us through."

"Of course," Euphrankes said. "Where do we stand on that?"

"With the Freethion you brought, and some of the Imperium, we should have enough to send a tracker load by the end of the week. I had Imperium on board that was never getting where it was headed, so we got a head start on you. I think we can make The Council very happy—apparently for the third time in a very short period. We're still going to need some supplies and support from them as well."

They rode in silence for a few moments more, and pulled up just short of the complex. The cargo passed them, moving around to a larger door. Lyones and Myklos took charge of the cargo, and Euphrankes went with Zins to take a look at the production that had gone on in his absence.

"We made a breakthrough on the mag drive," Zins told him excitedly. "We isolated the magnetic waves, and we managed to concentrate them. Slyphie did most of it, actually. She was able to create a beam about a thousand times as concentrated as you had in your prototype, and it increased the range astronomically."

Euphrankes turned with a grin.

"Then, you believe it will work? The mag drive? It's a pretty radical jump from how we navigate between the veils, but if we're right?"

"I'm sure it will work," Zins said. "We will see soon enough, I think. For now, we have to concentrate. A lot has been gained these past few days, but it could be as easily lost. We have to hold up our end and support Urv. If we do that, and if things open up between Urv and the outer cities, we'll be testing that mag drive together."

Euphrankes smiled.

"Who will take over the *Axis*, then? Surely you won't retire her."

"Termac will make a fine Captain," Zins said. "Can you imagine it? Even after seeing the *Tangent*, he would rather keep his boots closer to the First Veil. I don't pretend to understand how he can resist the urge to see what's out there, but I respect his decision. I'll be transferring all responsibility to him as soon as we have the cargo arranged. That is, if you'll have me on board?"

"We haven't the crew to handle the *Tangent* alone, and you know it," Euphrankes said. "I could use a Navigator, if you're interested? First Officer slot is taken, and Slyphie handles Engineering . . ."

"It sounds like a fine position for discovering the stars," Zins replied. "Consider it done. I will be sending most of my crew back out with Termac, but I suspect he will return with any remaining volunteers we need within the week. Word needs to be carried to the outlying cities, and I want him to get a start on that, but there's no reason he can't use this as a home base. We're also going to need a crew left behind here to handle the manufacture of the patches, and to reestablish communications and trade with Urv."

"There's more," Euphrankes said, staring out over the huge workroom, where already men and women were spreading out and digging in to the tasks at hand. "You are going to find this hard to believe, perhaps, but The High Councilor himself is somewhat of an engineer at heart."

Quickly, Euphrankes outlined High Councilor Cumby's design for a mobile, moveable seal that would allow work crews to pressurize the road behind them, and never be too far from safety as they moved out, repairing the damage to the great roads.

"It's brilliant!" Zins said. "This planet is slow to give up things like water and food, but there is no lack of metal or building materials. We can shore up those roads in no time, and with traffic restored, supplemented by the airships, it will be a new age. Families will reunite—business should prosper."

"And if the priests actually act as Cyril's words seem to indicate they might, the pumps may be cycling a lot more breathable air before long. Who knows, we may end up in the business of either manufacturing pumps, or at the very least, large pieces of them."

"It's going to be busy," Zins agreed. "I almost wish I was going to be here to see all of that, but . . ."

"I know," Euphrankes said with a grin. "Let's get out there and see if we can be of help without getting underfoot. We need—at the very least—to arrange the schedule to keep people working without anyone dropping off on us. We also have to prune out enough of a crew to take the tracker back through when the first cargo is ready."

They descended the stairs into the main workroom and split up, each heading for one or another group of workers.

The machinery was already in place to produce most of the parts for the patches. Euphrankes pulled Slyphie and Bonymede free of the process, which needed minimal supervision, and got them to work on designing the new mobile airlock. He assisted them until he was certain they had a good handle on what needed to be done, and then he slipped way and climbed up the tower to where the huge, hulking mass of the *Tangent* rested.

There were a few workers still busy on the hull. He waved to them as he passed on to the main airlock and sealed himself inside. He hadn't visited the ship since prior to his failed trip to Urv. It had only been a few days, but it already seemed like years. So much had changed and so much remained to be done. Only the bridge and the main engineering compartment had been pressurized. The *Tangent* had her own pumps, but they hadn't been brought online yet . . . what he breathed had to be cycled in from below, and it was a little thin.

To Euphrankes, it tasted like freedom. He stepped up to the Captain's seat, ran his hand over the polished wooden back, and stared out of the domed shield. It was not dark out yet, but it also wasn't light. The *Tangent* rested between the veils, so he could see the darkening sky opening up above him, and the tiny shapes of workers moving around the outer extremities of the main complex.

He heard a rustle behind him, but he didn't turn. A moment later, Aria's hands rested on his shoulder, and he leaned back into her as she wrapped her arms around him.

"It's still out there," she whispered in his ear. "It's not going anywhere."

"I know," he said. "I know it will be there when we're ready. It's waiting for us. I just have to come up here every now and then and watch it for a while. It's like I can feel it, some great mystery dragging at me and trying to lift me up into something brand new—something we can't even really conceive."

"I have some thoughts on conceiving," Aria whispered. She licked his ear lobe, and he shivered.

Euphrankes turned with a laugh and dragged her closer. She pressed into him eagerly.

"We spend so little time alone," she said. "I miss you."

"I know," he said, "and yet, once we take off, you may see more of me than you ever wanted to. It won't be like we can escape."

"That's a risk I'm willing to take," she said. She reached up and started to undo the buttons on his shirt.

"The door . . ." he gasped.

She silenced him with a single finger on his lips.

"Is sealed. I gave strict orders that we were not to be disturbed."

Euphrankes blushed slightly, thinking about whoever it was working out on the hull, and what they'd think of such an order. Then, as Aria slipped from her own work clothes and pressed him back into the ornate chair, all thoughts of those below slipped away. His vision was filled with her body, her eyes, and the endless stars stretching up behind her, calling them home.

CHAPTER EIGHTEEN

OVER THE NEXT SEVERAL WEEKS, both the tracker, and the *Axis*, came and went several times. Supplies, parts, and the first prototypes of the portable airlocks—fully tested on the road to Urv—were delivered, traded, bartered and presented. Though things had returned to a semblance of normalcy in Urv, there was no indication that The Council would back down on their new directives.

Zins, who flew with the *Axis* on her second voyage out of The Outpost, reported that the streets of the city were almost as busy as they'd been upon their last departure. There were crews currently working on all the roads out of Urv, and they had actually been required to hover for half a day to get a berth at the air towers. Rumor had it that High Councilor Cumby had commissioned the construction of a third tower with a larger airlock to be built as soon as all roads were complete, and the workers were available.

The air in the city had already increased in quality. Cyril had been as good as his word. Though there was still some resistance in The Temple, he'd begun a program to study the pumps. As yet, they had made only minor changes to their rituals, but they had managed to increase efficiency, and had located and replaced several parts that were on the verge of failure. There was also a small contingent of priests working to painstakingly recreate the manuals so that a copy could be presented to the city's engineers. The hope was that, with some time and patience, they might be able to machine parts to build more pumps and increase the breathable atmosphere in the city, the roads, and eventually throughout the range of the First Veil.

Priests had also been flying with the airships, reaching out to The Temples in the other cities. They had to spread the word that there was a new High Priest, and to pass on Cyril's changes to the rituals. Most of the other cities had already experienced more trouble with their pumps and air than Urv had and were happy to comply. Councilor Cumby believed that the few pockets of resistance would crumble once the roads were opened up. The entire world was changing, but Euphrankes, for all his involvement, felt detached from it.

He was focused on the *Tangent*. He'd spent nearly every waking moment on board the great ship, changing design criteria, working side-by-side with his own people and those of Zins' crew who'd been assigned to the task. Others had flown in—volunteers from different engineering disciplines and airship crews who'd heard of the great mission and wanted to be a part of it.

"We may actually have to draw straws to see who gets to accompany us through the veil," Euprhankes said.

He and Zins stood alone on the bridge of the *Tangent*. The interior was fully pressurized and the air was fresh and clean. They'd managed to use bits of design copied from Cyril's manual to improve on their designs, and now all that remained on the interior of the ship was the control and propulsion panels, and the wiring of the major systems. Everything gleamed. The metal was polished, every other surface was painted. She was a beautiful ship.

"It's a fool's mission," Zins said gruffly. "Everyone is probably going to die. They all know this. It's why they are so eager to sign on."

The two of them laughed softly.

"We're really going to do it," Euphrankes said. "We're going to pass through the Second Veil."

"And what will we find on the other side, do you think?" Zins asked. "I have found myself wondering this more and more as the day grows near. Slyphie estimates that the *Tangent* will be ready to fly within a week. After a shakedown between the veils, what then? Do you have a plan?"

Euprhankes shook his head. "We need to test the propulsion, and the range," he said. "Our telescopes are not powerful enough to reach much beyond our moons, and the nearest planets. My hope is that there will be other worlds that could sustain life—maybe even other cities and people we can learn from."

"And if they don't want to teach?" Zins asked. "If we only fly out to find barren rock, or worse yet, new enemies that will fall upon us and take what little we have?"

Euphrankes shook his head.

"That can't be all there is," he said. "All of this," he waved his arm to encompass the veils, the airship, the compound below, and the planet, "came from somewhere. At least one civilization much more advanced than ours has existed, and if they were the predators you speak of, they would hardly have put all of these protective measures in place."

"I'm not sure sometimes," Zins said, "if they are protections, or a cage. I hear what you're saying, though, and I agree. I'm just thinking out loud. I don't doubt that we will find something amazing out there, the only question is will we find it soon enough, and close enough, to do our planet any good."

Outside the view port they saw a shadow coming into view.

"The *Axis* is returning," Zins said. "They should have the last of the Imperium we need to be certain we're sealed in tight."

"Let's go and greet them," Euphrankes said. "I'd like to know what new things have happened in Urv since we last heard. It's been so many years since there was any good news at all that I find myself looking forward to it more than I would have believed."

They climbed down through the airlock and onto the platform. The *Axis* would dock at the next tower, but it would take half an hour or so to get her into position, so they had time. They climbed down and walked over from the base of one tower to the next. In the distance, the cargo carriers were rolling out of the complex and making their way slowly to the base of the tower.

By the time the airlock opened and the crew began their initial descent, half the workers in The Compound were gathered. When Lyones came down the ladder two rungs at a time, his hair wild around his head, they cleared the way for him. He ran straight to Euphrankes.

"You have to come!" he said. "You have to come to Urv. The Council gave the debris to the priests—to Cyril. You have to see what they've found."

"What . . ."

Lyones shook his head.

"I'm under oath to say nothing. You have to come. Frankes, it's important. Before you pass the veil, you need to see this."

Euphrankes turned to Zins in consternation. Zins shrugged.

"When can we be ready to leave?" Euphrankes asked.

"Dawn," Lyones said. "We have to unload the cargo, and it's full. It will take at least that long, and we'll need a crew. Can you go back and make preparations?"

"Why not take the *Vector*?" Zins asked. "We can fly that with a skeleton crew. She's been unloaded and waiting for more than a week. If we leave within the hour, we could be there by morning."

"Let's do it," Euphrankes said. "Let's get back to the complex. I'll get Aria, and Bonymede, and we can be back here within the hour.

"I'm going too," Zins said. "I wouldn't miss this for the world."

CHAPTER NINETEEN

THEY DOCKED AT URV'S MAIN air tower before sunrise. Despite the early hour, when they passed the airlock and climbed down, they were met by a small entourage of guards. None of The Councilors were present, but the guards explained they had orders to bring Euphrankes without delay.

They walked through the streets of city, and Euphrankes marveled at the changes. There was evidence of work—repair, and even some construction. Lights were on, and at this time of the morning, that was a thing that hadn't happened in Urv in a very long time.

"What's happened," Zins asked the guards. "What is so confounded important that we had to fly all night to get here?"

"I couldn't tell you," the guard said. "All I know is that the High Priest, Cyril, came here yesterday with a metal case. His eyes were wide, and he was almost running. He took that case into The Council Chamber, and they closed the doors. No one knows what they talked about. All we know is that when High Councilor Cumby opened the doors, he sent runners to catch the *Axis* before she took flight and to send her for you."

Zins turned to Euphrankes, who shrugged. They'd both seen the smoking, charred bit of machinery that had caused the damage to the veil, but it had been beyond their experience, and too damaged to make out. Euphrankes had figured it for a monument, or an artifact that would remind them of how close they'd come to disaster. Now it appeared they'd missed something.

As they climbed the steps to The Council Chamber, the doors opened, and Cumby stood framed, his hair askew and his eyes wild.

"Come with me," he said.

He turned then, and disappeared inside. Euphrankes and Zins exchanged a last look, and then, with Aria trailing behind, they hurried into the building and down the main hall. The doors to The Council Chamber stood open—another thing that Euphrankes, who had been there many times, had never seen before.

They entered the chamber and found the entire council gathered. Cyril was with them, and in the center of the main council table sat the box the guards had mentioned. Euphrankes wasted no time. He wasn't on trial this time or asking for favors. He'd been summoned. He hurried to the table, the others at his heels.

"What is it?" he asked without preamble. "What have you found?"

It was Cyril who stepped forward. He drew the box to one side of the table, and Euphrankes stepped up beside him. Zins and Aria crowded in on the other side. The box was lined with cloth, and in the center the artifact lay. It looked very different than it had the last time they'd seen it. For one thing, it had been disassembled. Instead of a charred chunk of circuits and metal, several long strips and a bit of casing rested in separate notches in the padding.

There were circuits clearly visible on the strips of strange material, and metal trails could be made out criss-crossing the surface. That was not what Cyril pointed to. On the case, faded and scorched, words had been written.

"What does it say?" Euphrankes asked, turning to Cyril.

"I have no idea," the priest replied, "but look here . . ."

He slapped a small book onto the table beside the crate. Euphrankes pulled his gaze away from the fragments of the artifact and stared at the book. It was one of the manuals for the pumps that had been pulled from the back of the forbidden locker. He could not read the lettering in the manual, either, though the diagrams were very clear. Then it hit him.

It wasn't an exact match, but there was no doubt that the letters and words printed on the artifact were a very close match for those printed in the manual. Euphrankes stared in shock, and then pushed the book across to Zins, and turned to Cyril.

"Oh my," he said. "This . . ."

"Yes, exactly," Cyril replied. The old priest's eyes were open wide and gleaming with excitement. "Whoever made this was associated with The Protectors."

"You think it was them?" Zins asked, glancing up from the manual. "Does anyone read this ancient text? Can we translate it?"

"We have tried," Cyril said. "The words don't make any sense, really. They may be names, or some sort of a brand. The letters are the same, but we can't find them repeated in the same pattern in any of the manuals. We can pronounce them—but we have no idea what we're saying."

"What about the artifact itself?" Aria asked. "Have you made any sense of it? Do you know what it does?"

Cyril shook his head.

"It's like nothing we've ever seen. It is made of unfamiliar materials. It's not a metal alloy, it's much weaker. It has a fiber content, and it is somewhat flexible. There are metal trails all over the surface that I suspect conducted signals, but with only this one small piece of the whole, we can't even make an educated guess at its purpose."

Euphrankes turned to Cumby.

"If it's them . . ."

"I know," Cumby said. "If this belonged to our protectors, then we have a good idea now why they have not come back to us, or given us further gifts of protection or technology. It also means, I think, that they are not the only beings or creatures or men, or whatever they are, that we are not aware of. Someone did this. Someone destroyed a thing so complex we can't even begin to understand it—and we have to wonder. What could such a force do to us? To the veils? What would they do?"

"They probably don't even know we exist," Zins said. "It has been so long since The Protectors acknowledged this planet that it seems likely we are as much a legend to them at this point as they are to us."

"Or," Cyril said, his voice soft, but carrying, "they are still protecting us. If they have not reached out to us, perhaps it is so that their communications could not be intercepted. If we are forgotten, it buys us time."

"Time for what?" Cumby said.

"To prove ourselves worthy," Zins said without hesitation. "To find ways to defend ourselves, and to survive, without the help of protectors looking out for us. To reach out and know our enemies, prepare for them, and do our best."

"And if that best isn't good enough?" Councilor Illana cut in, "what then?"

"Then nothing," Zins replied with a shrug. "We are apparently getting closer to encountering whoever did this," he waved at the case on the table, "whether we prepare or not. I'm thinking they aren't the talking kind. We can ready ourselves for the day they finally find us, or we can ignore it and go on and hope our children have to deal with it, but none of it will change the danger. It is entirely up to us."

Cumby glanced around the room.

"In a very real way, what Maester Zins has said is true. This is the room where decisions are made. We are the men, and women, who will decide what road we take into the future. If we are destroyed, it will be at least in part because we ourselves have failed. I see no real way to protect ourselves, and I'm not optimistic about our chances if we are discovered . . . but neither am I willing to roll over and let our world be consumed by some distant darkness we don't understand."

Euphrankes had pulled a small book from a pocket of his protective suit. He leaned in close over the table and studied the artifact carefully. Then, with careful strokes, he copied down the letters from the metal plate.

Lockhe d—that was all he could make out. There was more in the middle, but he thought if they encountered anyone who was familiar with such characters along the way, they could show it to them. It might mean something, it might not. It might make them friends, or enemies. There was no way to know whether they would first encounter the creators of whatever had been destroyed, or the destroyers. There was no way, even, to know which side—ultimately—had been in the right.

"I'm trying to figure out what could destroy something so completely," Aria said, frowning. "I mean, I know there must be weapons out there far beyond anything we've seen, but . . ."

"It's the veils," Zins said. "We have limited weapons technology, but it isn't because we couldn't create something much more destructive. Think of the mag drives we've just finished, directed on the surface of a building, or a ship, not for the purpose of propelling an airship, but to pull it apart magnetically."

"You have thought about such things?" Euphrankes asked, turning to his old friend in shock.

"Since the moment I believed you could really propel us up and beyond the veils, yes." Zins replied. "How can you not? If we get out there and find whoever destroyed that," he pointed at the table, "we'd better be prepared in case they have similar plans for us, don't you think? Otherwise, what is the point in going at all?"

They were all silent for a few moments, and then Cumby spoke.

"I believe Maester Zins is correct. You are going to have to bend some of the brilliance you have available to you toward defenses, and weapons. You can't go blindly out there and hope that the universe is a wonderful place. Judging from how things can go wrong in a closed environment like Urv, I think we can guess how they might go on a grander scale."

"We've already got plans," Zins said softly. "We haven't shown you yet, Frankes . . . and I'm sorry for that, but we knew you'd be opposed, and we didn't want to leave this work all for the last moment."

Euphrankes reached out then and ran a hand over the jagged edge of the fragment of machinery on the table. He glanced up at Zins.

"You are right, I am opposed, but I am also not a fool. Everything you and the High Councilor have said is true. I ask only that we spend more time on defensive systems . . . Imperium is a powerful shield, and that same magnetic field you envision as an offensive weapon could create an interesting shield, with some modifications."

Zins smiled.

"Of course . . . we'll show you what we have on the return trip, and we can make plans for incorporating it into the *Tangent*'s design."

"How close are you?" Cyril asked curiously. "How soon might you attempt to pass the veil?"

"We can be ready in a matter of a couple of weeks," Euphrankes said. "The construction for the patches and portable airlocks is nearly automated. We have split our crews among those who wish to join us on the *Tangent*, and those who want to remain behind and man the compound, helping as they can to reopen the roads and pilot the airships between cities. We need only a few more for the journey."

"I wish that I could go," Cyril said wistfully. "I wish that I could see these wonderful machines you are building and pass the veils. I wish that I could join you on a journey that may, in the end, bring you face to face with The Protectors, or those like them. All my life I've been worshipping them. Now, just on the verge of realizing that they are not omnipotent protectors, but very possibly men not so unlike myself, I find that knowing is suddenly very important.

"Do we have a method of communication designed?" he asked. "How will we know what you find, or discover? How far will we go before you return?"

Euphrankes grinned.

"Slyphie figured out the communications. She has had some considerable success bouncing signals off of objects beyond the veil—very distant objects—using yet another application of mag theory. This planet is—as you know—riddled with veins and pockets of metal. It is possible, using rods pounded deep into the surface of the planet, to use that metal as an antenna of sorts. We've been working on a receiver. So far, all it's picked up is noise . . . scattered bursts of radiation from beyond the veil. With the transmitter we have designed, however, we should be able to beam signals directly back to that receiver from very great distances.

"We'll need someone to monitor that signal, Cyril," he said softly. "Do you suppose you could find room in The Chamber of Stars for it? I can think of no more appropriate place . . ."

Cyril's eyes grew bright.

"Of course!" he said at once. "I will send priests with you to help bring it to Urv and install it!"

"We'll keep a second receiver at The Outpost as backup," Euphrankes said. "We haven't figured out a way yet that you can send signals back to the *Tangent*, but you will be able to receive regular reports on our progress, and on any discoveries we make."

"And I will continue to study the artifact, and the pumps," Cyril said. "We will work with your engineers—perhaps we'll discover a means of sending back a signal on our own. Be certain you install a receiver on board the *Tangent*, as well as just a transmitter."

"Done," Euphrankes said.

"I think we'd better get back to The Outpost," Zins said. "Seeing this artifact again, and wondering, has me on edge."

"Agreed," Euphrankes said.

"Thank you for coming so quickly," Cumby said. "I will feel better knowing The Temple has a means of following your progress. I have to admit, if I didn't have so many years under my belt, I'd be tempted to tag along myself. I've spent a very long time cooped up in this place."

"It's not just the veils that are opening up," Zins said. "The roads will be clear soon, and I'm thinking it's been far too long since representatives of The Council reached out to the remote cities in person."

"Perhaps you are right," Cumby said. "The travel would certainly do my spirits good."

"Then we will see you soon," Euphrankes said. "Maybe you can make the trip to The Outpost to see us off on our journey."

"It would be an honor," Cumby said.

"Then," Euphrankes said, shaking the old man's hand for the second time in less than a month, "we will see you there."

The group broke up then. Cyril carefully closed the case and carried it out of the chamber. Euphrankes, Zins, and Aria returned to the air towers, and High Councilor Cumby—with an escort of his guards—trailed along to watch them depart.

As the *Vector* pulled away from the air dock and floated into the distance, he spoke quietly to himself.

"Hurry, Euphrankes. Get out there, and find them. I would very much like to live to see it."

CHAPTER TWENTY

"WE'VE MADE CONTACT," ARIA CALLED out.

She sat on the far side of the *Tangent*'s bridge from Euphrankes, a microphone in one hand and a polished brass headset, the earpieces manufactured to attach to the leather-covered helmet of her protective suit, perched on her head. The cable it was attached to had twin plugs that snaked into the single cable leading to the earpiece and attached at the other end to a pair of radios. One radio was hooked into the standard radio frequency that linked the cities—spotty, but better since they'd raised the antennas to place them between the veils. Signals transmitted better in the thinner atmosphere, and they were able to bounce around the curved surface of the planet by using the reflective qualities of the Second Veil.

The other cable plugged into the new gear. They'd been working with it furiously, trying to get it operational before launch.

"The Temple reads you, then?" Euphrankes asked.

"Loud and clear," she beamed. "Now I'm going to test the receiver on this end."

"It should work fine here," Euphrankes said. "The question

is, shooting through the Second Veil, how far can they send a signal—when will we lose them?"

Aria nodded absently. She flipped a large toggle switch, adjusted the cables and spoke into the microphone again. She sat, intent on whatever she heard through the headset, and Euphrankes watched her for a reaction. At first she frowned, and he feared they weren't going to get a response. Then Aria smiled, and Euprhankes couldn't help the grin that spread across his own face.

"It's good," she said. "I don't know if it will work past the veils, but we have a clear connection on the new equipment."

"Let's keep regular reports, twice daily, from here out," Euphrankes said. "That way we get a good chance to let the equipment burn in, and to check for bugs. We won't have much time to adjust it once we're gone. We need a solid connection from the start, and we have to maintain it. I assume our own transmissions to Urv will get through, but there's nothing like knowing for certain—and the only way to know is to get a response."

"Slyphie has added another bit to it," Aria said. She indicated a red light on the side of the receiver. "Watch this."

She spoke into the microphone again. This time she smiled more quickly as the response came directly back. As she did, the red light blinked three times, and then grew steady again.

"What does it mean?" Euphrankes asked.

"It means we received a response," Aria said. "It will detect a signal much too small for actual voice translation, but will tell us that Urv has acknowledged our transmission. As long as we see that light blink, we know we got through. There are codes as well. If it goes off and stays off for a moment, it means our transmission was received but garbled. If it starts beeping constantly, they have received nothing in more than a day and are asking us to please respond with a status."

"That's wonderful," Euphrankes said.

He turned back to the console before him. They'd run a thousand simulations, and the mag drive appeared as if it would function as they expected it to. It didn't change the risk, or the fact that an entire crew of men and women would be trusting him with their lives as they launched into the unknown. He wished there was a more real-world way to test it, but he'd done all that he could.

"We will be ready in two, maybe three days," he said.

Aria glanced over at him.

"We are ready now," she said. "We will soon have to quit putting it off and cut the lines."

Euphrankes looked as though he might argue, thought better of it, and chuckled. "You are right, of course. We have to make this a reality. It will no longer be enough to dream."

"Have you made the final selections for the crew?" she asked. "Zins was waiting on that so he could begin scheduling watch duty, and assign berths."

"It is nearly there," Euphrankes said. "There are two slots still uncertain. It's as hard to turn anyone away from this mission as it is to accept them, knowing the uncertainty of the outcome. The selfish part of me wants to just go myself, see if I survive, and come back, but that can't happen. It's a lot of responsibility."

"It's not all yours," Aria said. "You know that. They want to go . . . WE want to go, and it's not a question any longer of should we—we need answers."

"I know, I know," Euphrankes said. "It doesn't make it any easier to sleep at night."

Aria laughed. "One of these days, you'll drop dead of worrying about others."

"Great," Euphrankes said, finally smiling and letting out a chuckle. "Now I'll have to worry about dropping dead and letting everyone down."

Aria shook her head and turned back to the radio sets. She chatted with Cyril in Urv for a few moments, setting up a schedule for regular broadcasts and responses. Euphrankes puttered about the bridge, checking and rechecking instruments and equipment that had already been gone over a hundred times. Everything was gleaming metal and shined to brilliance. There were familiar controls, and brand new ones that had never been tested.

The maiden voyage, a between the veils flight to Urv, was scheduled for that evening. Euphrankes hadn't slept. He hadn't slept well in over a week, in fact. He kept thinking about the stars, and the vast, dark spaces surrounding them. He thought about the debris, and the type of destruction that could send such a thing hurtling through space to their doorstep.

He glanced over at Aria again.

"Their planet could have just exploded," he said. "There might not be a threat at all, other than a natural one. There may be nothing to find."

She looked over at him and frowned.

"You don't believe that. If you did, we wouldn't have spent the last week perfecting and testing weapons. We have never built a weapon in all the years of my life—not here, not in Urv. The idea that we may need them, and that our lack of knowledge in that area may be our greatest weakness is the one thing, of all those you worry about too much, that troubles me as well.

"What kind of man—or being—destroys things like that? We

squabble and banish one another, and we've even had skirmishes between cities. We've never had a conflict on any greater level, though. There has always been the knowledge behind it all that anything we do can affect the veils. Do you think it's possible that this is the gift The Protectors have given us?"

"What do you mean?" Euphrankes asked.

"We take nothing for granted. Our homes, our cities, our roads—the air that we breathe. Our laws, our ways, and our lives are built around preserving those things. We hold the preservation of life above all other things; it's ingrained in our culture. Maybe The Protectors have seen too many destructive peoples. Maybe this was a way of molding us into protectors. In a universe that may be filled with fighting on a large scale, we may be the calming factor."

"It's a pleasant thought," Euphrankes mused. "The trouble is that—if it's true—then that means most other races won't share our concerns with preserving life. We may not get the opportunity to explain ourselves, or to influence anyone, before we're blown out of the sky to become strange debris on someone else's doorstep."

They worked on in silence. It was two hours before launch, and the others had begun entering the airlock and slipping on board.

"I have to go below," Euphrankes said. "I have to choose the final two crewmembers, and there's no sense putting it off any longer."

Aria nodded.

"I'm going to find Slyphie and record the schedule that Cyril and I have established. We'll choose a small group to be responsible around the clock for the transmission, and for recording any messages from the surface."

"I'll be bringing the main log with me when I return," Euphrankes said. "We'll keep that here on the bridge. All command level personnel will have access when on watch. I have the feeling it may be one of the most important and fascinating things written in the planet's history. I brought a lot of ink."

Aria laughed.

"Perhaps," she said, "I should schedule a daily recital of the entries over the radio? Cyril could record them and they'll know what's happening to us. Even if we get too far out of range for him to respond, we'll be able to leave a record."

"That is a wonderful idea," Euphrankes said. "Imagine that. After all the trouble we've caused, and all the years of exile, there might be one of those fabulous, thick-spined books in The Chamber of Stars with our words in it."

"I can see the title now," Aria laughed. "The Voyages of the *Tangent*: Captain Euphrankes Holymnn."

"More like the adventures of the crew of the airship *Tangent*," Euphrankes said, "led by some guy who had no idea what he was doing."

"Just so Myril doesn't break out of confinement to write a sequel titled 'I told you so,' I'm okay with that," Aria said.

They both laughed.

"I'll be back in an hour," Euphrankes said. "Get everyone ready for the launch. We'll meet in the main dining hall right before we leave. Don't know if I've got an inspirational speech in me, but I'll give it my best shot. I suspect there will be some sort of festivities for our arrival and sendoff in Urv as well. We're celebrities, you know. We might as well enjoy it while we can."

"We'll be ready," she said. Then, with a flip of her hair and a laugh, she added, "Skipper."

With a heavy sigh, Euphrankes turned and headed for the airlock. He couldn't escape the fluttering sensations in the pit of his stomach, but he wasn't frightened. He just wondered if he'd be able to stand the hours left before they turned the nose of the *Tangent* toward space and launched into a new world.

Chapter Twenty-One

THE CREW WAS GATHERED AROUND the oval table in the main dining hall. Some had to take up seats along the walls—the hall was designed for them to eat in shifts. There were twelve members of the crew. Euphrankes, Zins, and Aria made up the command. Ozymandes was to serve as an engineer, and as the ship's chaplain, should anyone have second thoughts, or want to talk about The Protectors, or the lore of their own planet. He took both roles very seriously, and was particularly pleased to have been chosen to be among those allowed access to the ship's log, and to be part of the communications rotation.

Euphrankes stood at the head of the table. He had a seat, but he could no more have sat down in it at that moment than he could have flown without the ship. His nerves were on edge, and his eyes were bright. If he still had doubts, they were absent from his words and his expression. He paced back and forth, studying each of those gathered.

"What we are about to do," he said at last, "has been described to me over the past few weeks as remarkable, foolish, courageous, and suicidal."

There was a smattering of nervous laughter, but there was

too much possible truth in every one of the descriptions to laugh too hard.

"I prefer to think of it," Euphrankes continued, "as an aspect of destiny. Everything we are—everything we've done, studied, figured out, argued about and lived has brought us here to this moment. Together. There isn't one among you who has not contributed their part, and we haven't even left dock. Before we are done, I suspect we will all have our chances to explore whether we are courageous, mad, foolish, or a strange combination of all of the above.

"Everything we experience will be new. We have studies and theories, but in the end, that is all we have until we pass the Second Veil. Once we are in space, where we believe it to be a vacuum without atmosphere, that is when we will begin to actually learn. From that moment forward, we will observe, record, and experience facts. We have to be quick and clever. We have to be able to assimilate what we find and encounter, and learn from it on the fly. There is no experience to fall back on, and in many cases we may discover there are no second chances.

"That said, if there are any among you having second thoughts about making this voyage, now is the time to speak. I will ask this question one more time, when we are moored in Urv. After that, we are committed, every one of us, to this adventure. The very future of our planet may depend on what we find, how we react to it, report it, and adapt. Are you ready for that responsibility?"

There was a subdued murmur of assent. Every face was serious, but Euphrankes saw his own eagerness to be underway mirrored on every face. He had studied and worried over the choices for the crew, and now, seeing them assembled and ready to fly, he smiled. They were the best of the best. All of those he'd most wanted to have with him had come, and the few who he'd not counted on, like the young priest Ozymandes, had proven invaluable already.

Oz, as they'd begun to call him after only a single day of working with him, had a very quick mind when it came to mechanical engineering. He also had years of practice drawing, recording, and "ritualizing" maintenance procedures. Since the *Tangent* was new and many of her systems would be tested for the first time under fire, it was good to have someone along with a background of and tendency toward careful, practical procedure.

Zins would serve as navigator, officially, but Euphrankes knew the man could be counted on in any capacity. He wasn't an engineer, but he could fly an airship, and he could lead. When things got tough and it was impossible to be in enough places at one time to keep an emergency under control, Zins would be another version of himself. It would also be good to have him for conversation, once they were alone in space. They shared dreams and visions, and Zins had known Euphrankes' father.

They'd also ended up with a good mix of men and women. They didn't necessarily want to encourage deep relationships between crew members, but Euphrankes had Aria, and he knew that if they'd brought only men, or only women, eventually trouble would ensue. There had to be some semblance of normalcy, and there was just no way to gauge how far they'd be traveling, or how long they'd be gone.

Food was somewhat of a problem, but this time it was Bonymede who'd come through with a solution. In a chamber near the rear of the ship he'd rigged a second dome, not as large as that they used to navigate on the bridge, but sufficient to catch light from suns and stars. Rigged up around that chamber were powerful lights, aimed at an array of narrow rows of planters.

One of the mysteries of The Protectors was where the first seeds had come from, and how the equipment they used in the cities to drill into the planet's surface to find and sift the proper soil and chemical mixtures to grow the food that kept them alive. There wasn't much variety to it, but it sustained, and Bonymede had created a miniature garden in the image of one of the larger plantations. He had soil, and enough chemicals to enrich it when necessary.

Cyril had presented them with one of the miraculous distillation machines that created the water they drank. No one had even begun to fathom how these worked. The cities recycled everything. Water, waste, and air were reconstituted by great machines. Certain chemicals drawn up by the same drills that produced their soil were shifted over to the distillation plants, combined with the city's waste, filtered and distilled, and provided a seemingly endless stream of fresh water.

What Cyril had given them was a very small version of one of the distillers, and several tanks of chemicals. Bonymede had tied it all together with the ship's waste management system, and—by all indications—they could produce more water and food than they should be able to use, allowing them to store and hoard supplies. All of it was miraculous—Oz's word for it. Every possible trouble that Euphrankes' fertile imagination could invent, someone on the crew, or in the cities, or at The Compound, found a solution for.

"I am proud to fly with you," Euphrankes said at last. "Every one of you. I spoke a few moments ago about destiny. Look around you at all we have created. Think about the things that stood between us and success, and how this crew—this small group of individuals—grew into a single powerful force to overcome them."

He stood for a moment as his words sank in, and then went on.

"Okay, everyone to your posts. Strap in. Get the lines cleared, and be certain the ground crews are ready. We will launch for Urv in ten minutes."

Without another word, he turned and headed back up toward the bridge. The others rose quickly, glad to have a purpose, and glad to have a few moments to think, not only about what Euphrankes had said, but about the short journey to come, and the much longer one in the near future.

None of them said it, but they were all proud to serve under Euphrankes. Even those who'd been with Zins before, or who'd never served on a crew of any kind. His enthusiasm was infectious, and his confidence that they were doing the right thing inspired them.

They spread out through the ship, setting controls and releasing moorings. Slyphie and Bonymede slowly decompressed Freethion into the membranes surrounding them and very gently they lifted to the length of the few remaining restraints. Engineers below decoupled the airlocks, dropping back through and sealing the locks behind themselves, glancing up through protective helmets at the bottom of the *Tangent*'s huge hull.

The ship was easily twice the size of the *Vector* or any other airship they'd manufactured in the past. It was long and sleek, less oval and more cylindrical. The hull was reinforced by Imperium straps around the outside of the already nearly impenetrable Imperium hull. Every inch of the ship glistened, and as it pulled away from its moorings and drifted up toward the Second Veil, those below thought it was like a great, silver star in the sky.

Then the ship leveled off, spun lazily, and started off toward Urv, gaining speed. Euprhankes put the ship and the crew through their paces, intent on shaking out any bugs before they reached their destination.

In only a few moments, The Outpost shrank to the size of a small child's toy, and then winked out of sight.

CHAPTER TWENTY-TWO

WHEN THE TANGENT REACHED URV, they found a huge gathering of citizens waiting for them at the base of the main air tower. A new system of airlocks had been installed, larger, to allow cargo transfer, like those at The Outpost, and modified for the *Tangent*'s locks so that the much larger ship could moor at a slightly greater height than the smaller ships. The changes represented a lot of work, and Euphrankes was impressed.

The difference in Urv was astonishing. Things that had seemed grimy, forgotten, and on the short track to entropy were clean, polished, and gleamed in the morning light. The streets were cleared, and there were even a few vehicles moving about them.

"Word has it," Zins said, staring down at those gathered below, "that the main road to Bethes has been cleared. They've made it through with a large cargo of food, and the priests in Bethes are working with Cyril's ambassadors to strengthen their pumps. The air is a little better all along, and people are coming outside to enjoy it."

"It's surreal," Euphrankes said. "I feel like it's only been days since I climbed down from this same platform, only to be banished for daring to dream about the ship I'm standing in now."

"That's the way life works," Zins said with a shrug. "When things happen, they tend to happen suddenly. It could have been a lot different outcome . . . I'd say we did pretty good."

Euphrankes smiled.

"You're right, of course. Doesn't change how it feels, though. I still can't get used to the idea of High Councilor Cumby smiling."

Both men laughed, and then, as the final lock was clamped in place, they preceded the crew down through the airlocks and onto the platform. As he climbed down, Euprhankes heard something odd. The lower he got, the louder the sound grew, and then very suddenly he recognized it. It was music. Live music.

He stopped and glanced down. Zins, who was descending directly behind him, nearly stepped on his head.

"What is it?" Zins asked, irritated.

"Listen," Euphrankes said.

And they did. All of them, up and down the ladder. They stood very still, and they listened, and then, suddenly someone laughed. It wasn't a laugh of mirth, but of delight.

"Where is it coming from?" Zins asked.

"I'm not sure," Euphrankes said. "Let's get down there and find out."

At the base of the tower, they found their answer. Cyril was there, and with him was a small contingent of priests. Each of them held a different instrument. Euphrankes had heard the music before, of course. They played it in The Temple nightly. None of them, however, had ever seen the men with the instruments—and, in his memory, the music had never been played in the streets.

High Councilor Cumby stepped forward with Cyril by his

side. The old priest was smiling.

"Don't look so shocked," he said. "When I was a boy— and granted, that was a very long time ago—there was often music in the streets. We've been playing as often as we can, even working on some new songs. The sound seems to help the workers, and the air . . . it's been a long time since it was better to breathe outside The Temple than it is inside. Since we have you to thank . . ."

Euphrankes held up a hand.

"Stop that," he said. "There were a lot of people involved in bringing about these changes. I may have helped to set it all in motion but without the two of you supporting me, and my crew, and Zins' crew, and . . . well . . . let's say it's been a group effort. The music is lovely."

They all stood for a while and listened. Finally, High Councilor Cumby broke the silence.

"They have a small ceremony planned in your honor," he said, "all of you. The citizenry and The Council and even The Temple have a few things to gift you. I know you can't carry much, but I think you'll find that what we have will be of use. Then we'll settle you all in for a good night's rest to be ready for tomorrow's launch."

Euphrankes nodded. He couldn't resist glancing up over his shoulder into the sky.

They walked back toward Urv as a group. Some things had not changed. They still didn't use mechanized transport lightly. Cumby explained that they wanted to maintain as much order as possible, so they were not changing the rules en masse. Also, they felt that the revitalized atmosphere didn't need to be challenged so soon. The attitude of the citizens, and The Council, was that the improvements were a blessing, and to be treated as such.

The walk seemed somehow shorter than the last time they'd made it. The way was lined with waving, cheering citizens, and the priests and their instruments followed along behind. Before they knew it, they were in the city proper, where they saw that tables had been set up in the street outside The Council Hall. There were banners and baskets, food and drink.

On the central table there was a pile of packages. The rest of The Council sat behind in chairs behind that table, arranged in a semi-circle. There was a podium fronting the chairs, and High Councilor Cumby made his way to it slowly. Euphrankes and the others stood, uncertain what to expect, waiting.

"This is too weird," Aria whispered. "Has The Council ever met outside the chamber before this?"

"There were times, long ago, when they did," Euphrankes said. "I've never seen it, but my father told me they used to hold ceremonies where they honored those who accomplished great things, and made presentations. When Myril became High Priest there was such a ceremony.

Once Cumby was in place, the group was ushered up to stand across the table from him, turned so that they faced out into the crowd. Hundreds of faces smiled back at them, some that they knew, others they'd never seen. There were children clinging to their parent's legs and couples, arm-in-arm. They stood and waited as Cumby turned on the amplifier on his podium and cleared his throat.

"It has been too long since we have gathered like this," he said. "The last time, I was a much younger man, and the occasion was less auspicious. I hope that in the future we'll have occasion to do this often. With the roads opening, and new breakthroughs in the pumps, patches, and airlocks daily,

I suspect it won't be a problem to find those worthy of reward.

"Today, there is no doubt of the occasion. By this time tomorrow, some of our best and brightest will be launched on a new adventure. I can't begin to tell you all that may be riding on their success, and I don't believe I have to tell you the danger they face. It is a courageous mission, and one worthy of The Protectors, who made it possible for us to survive and progress to this point . . . often against our will."

There was a polite smattering of applause, but it was subdued. None of them was quite comfortable with the new order, and laughing at the way they'd lived their lives for decades did not come easily.

"Before we send them off," Cumby continued, "The Council, some of our engineers, and the priests of The Temple have gathered a few items to send along with them. We realize that space is limited, so we have prepared nothing to large or ungainly, but I believe what we have will be of some use, and possibly some comfort before all is said and done.

"Euphrankes, Zins, Aria, would the three of you step up here please?"

They did as they were asked, standing at the table. There were five packages, neatly wrapped. They were not marked for any particular person. The labels read:

To the Officers and Crew of the *Tangent*.

Farscinian, a thin, darkly mustached Councilor, rose from his seat and stepped up to face them across the table. He picked up the first of the packages and presented it to Euphrankes.

"This first is my personal gift to you, Euphrankes," High Councilor Cumby said. "It is addressed to the entire crew, because I trust you will display it in a place where it can provide inspiration and hope. It was presented to The Council by your father, long, long ago. I believe you may recognize it, or, at least what it represents."

Euphrankes opened the package carefully. When the paper fell to the table, he held a small, transparent case. Inside, resting on delicately constructed metal blocks, was a model of an airship. The lines were much older than those of the *Vector*, very similar to those of the *Axis*. Euphrankes stared at it for a long time, and then glanced up sharply.

"This is the model he brought before The Council? The one he used . . ."

"To convince us that he should be allowed to put an airlock in the First Veil and build an airship. Yes, Euphrankes . . . that is the prototype model for the *Alexis* . . . sister ship to Maester Zins' *Axis*."

Euprhankes held the case very carefully. He studied the tiny airship, and a tear formed at the corner of one of his eyes. He didn't wipe it away, and eventually it trickled down his cheek and dropped to the ground.

"Thank you," he said at last. "I will mount this on the bridge of the *Tangent* in a place where all who pass will see it."

Cumby nodded, and smiled. Next, Councilor Farscinian picked up a longer, flatter package and held it out to Maester Zins, who took it with a small bow.

"As Navigator," Cumby said, "you will be responsible for the charts. We weren't sure what you had available, or how accurate they might be, so we've had the priests on watch in The Chamber of Stars kept busy This package contains charts of the stars as we know them, and duplicate copies so you will be able to record your travels more accurately. They are bound for protection, and we would be honored if, upon your return, you would return them to the library in that chamber for study."

"I will keep them carefully," Zins said, bowing again, "and I will return them gladly. It would be an honor to have my words kept in so important a collection."

The next package was much smaller, and Farscinian offered it to Aria.

"I know that as First Officer, you won't be spending a lot of time in the gardens," Cumby said, "but it will be your job to interface with the crew, and to help keep morale as high as possible. With the opening of the road to Bethes, we've been able to renew certain stores that have been lacking for a long time. This package contains several varieties of seeds. If used properly, and tended well, they will help add variety to your meals, and help to bring a few smiles. I hear that you have a rather remarkable gardening setup on board. I trust you can make good use of them."

"I will carry these to Bonymede, who designed the gardens and lighting system," Aria said. "I will personally see that they are cared for properly, and I thank you. On such a long journey, any distraction will be important, and a variety in the menu will be perfect."

There were two packages left. Farscinian picked the first and handed it to Euphrankes.

"In the way of distractions, we don't have all that much to offer," Cumby said. "What we have, though, is yours. This gift is also from the priests. They have copied several volumes from their library—a history of Urv, an observation log of the stars, which you will find also includes notes, thoughts, and writings by priests stretching back a very great amount of time into the city's past. Many of them are inspirational. Also included is a collection of stories written by citizens of Urv over the years. Many such have been penned, as you know, but these, over time, were gathered and deemed worthy of preservation. I hope they will remind you of family, and home."

It was Euphrankes turn to bow. It was a great honor. Books were simply not lent from the library of The Temple. They were kept as the private provenance of the priests, studied and meditated on—often read aloud in The Temple. The act of copying such a work involved many long hours of labor, and it was a great gift.

"Finally," Cumby said, "I have something we promised you earlier—something more practical. It is our hope that you will pass this on to young Ozymandes for safekeeping and study. In this package you will find copies of all the manuals associated with the pumps. Since you will be transmitting to us regularly, it is our hope that, should you discover anything of significance, you will pass that along to us as well. In the meantime, we thought the diagrams and rituals might aid you in improving your own systems and keep you that much safer until you return."

Euphrankes placed the packages safely on the table, and turned to face the crowd. He didn't have a microphone, so he spoke loudly and as clearly as he could. He found it difficult at first because of the odd lump that had formed in his throat.

"Tomorrow," he said, "we'll launch into an unknown future. Not that many years in the past, though it seems lifetimes, my father took such a leap of faith, and because of that, we have the airships. I would like to think that, were he here, he'd approve of what we're doing.

"There is a lot of work to be done right here in Urv, in the roads, and in neighboring cities. This is a great time for all of us—a coming together. For too many years we've allowed our world, our families, our cities—to grow farther apart. We've accepted things as they came, rather than working toward change.

"Now change of a higher magnitude has been thrust upon us. We have come to levels of understanding that serve only to show us how little we actually understand. It's a frightening, glorious, intriguing, wonderful time to be alive. We will think of each and every one of you as we launch, and we will send back what we can. We will find new answers—probably to questions we haven't even thought of yet.

"The future is a place worth going," he concluded. "We thank you for the thoughts, and the gifts. I only hope we prove worth of all the hope, gifts, and good wishes."

There was scattered applause, and Euphrankes waved, smiling.

"That concludes the presentations," Cumby said. "We have refreshments available, and we hope our enterprising voyagers will mingle, speak to us and answer questions for a time. We don't want to keep them too late. I've arranged good, comfortable quarters for the entire crew so they can leave refreshed, rested, and as comfortable as possible."

There was a light squeal of feedback from the amplifier, and then the crowd began milling nervously forward. Euphrankes, Zins, and Aria greeted them, talking, laughing, listening to the thoughts and dreams of each crowd member and doing their best to make the moment as memorable for those gathered as it had been for them.

Finally things began to break up, and Euphrankes gathered his companions. They scooped up the gifts they'd been presented. Cumby directed them to follow him, into The Council building.

"We have arranged quarters here," he said. "We have rooms that, in the past, were used by visiting dignitaries from distant cities. We hope to make use of them again in the near future, and this was a good opportunity to freshen them and get them ready."

"We appreciate every bit of this," Euphrankes said. "We would have been fine on board, of course, but this will be more comfortable, and will give us a solid, final memory of the city."

"We'll see you in the morning," Cumby said with a smile. "I'll escort you back to the tower. I think most of The Council will be gathered with Cyril in the Chamber of Stars to watch your departure. They have a young artist who will be present, as well . . . they hope he'll be able to record the moment with more clarity than memory alone could manage."

The men all shook hands, and in a completely unexpected gesture, Cumby gave Aria a quick, tight hug.

"Sleep well," he said. "And Euphrankes, your words will be remembered. 'The future is, indeed, a place worth visiting.' I will not forget you said that."

Cumby turned then and walked away, leaving them with two of the guards, who escorted them to their rooms for the night. It was not long before they separated into their quarters and climbed into bed.

Euphrankes and Aria took advantage of the spacious quarter afforded them. They wrapped themselves in one another's arms and made slow, careful love until they fell asleep in a jumble of arms, legs and dreams. They slept deeply, well, and long, awakening only when a soft beeping from the room's communicator summoned them to their morning meal.

"What do you think?" Aria asked sleepily. "Ready to meet the future?"

"As long as it's with you," Euphrankes answered, rolling off the bed and dressing quickly. "Anywhere, as long as it's with you."

CHAPTER TWENTY-THREE

RESTED AND WELL-FED, THE CREW gathered in the street outside The Council hall at daybreak. Despite the hour, the streets were filled with citizens. Some had brought small items—gifts to be taken back to the *Tangent*. There was no way they could take it all, but they accepted it anyway, knowing that some would be left behind at the air-tower. There were books, notes and letters, small keepsakes, and a lot of well-wishes.

They took it all in good grace, though a bit befuddled by all the attention. Finally they started out through the town, moving in the center of a formation of guards. No one believed they were in any danger, but if they hadn't had the escort, they might not have forced their way through the crowd at all. As it was, their progress was orderly.

The air tower was surrounded as well, and at the center the priests and The Council had gathered once more. It was more subdued than the previous day's festivities, but there was still an air of quiet excitement hanging over the crowd. The anticipation was palpable. No one knew exactly what they would see . . . most knew that they'd witness only the initial liftoff. Only those who made their way back to The Chamber of Stars in time would actually witness the passing of the veil.

It didn't matter. They understood the gravity of what was taking place, and they wanted to be part of it. When it came time to tell the tale, whether that tale was of brave travelers breaking into space, or plunging to their deaths, they wanted to be able to say that when it happened, they were there. Most of them didn't grasp all that was involved, or understand fully what had happened to the wall of the city—but they knew things had suddenly gotten better. It was the first major change in their lives for decades.

Euphrankes was aware of all of it, but his mind was already on the bridge, and his fingers twitched for the controls of the *Tangent*. He barely heard the short speeches, and though he knew he had shaken hundreds of hands, he was later able to remember only a few faces and names. The others each dealt with it in their own way. Zins enjoyed the attention, and Aria spent most of her time staying close to Euphrankes and running interference when the crowds came too close, or seemed ready to overwhelm him.

At last they mounted the ladder, and to the cheers of the citizens of Urv, climbed up to the platform above. Euphrankes was last to go, and before he started up, High Councilor Cumby placed a hand on his shoulder. The two faced one another for a last moment.

"I know I've not made your life an easy one," Cumby said, "and for that I'm sorry. Still, it is times like this that I wonder—if anything had happened differently along the way, would we have made it to this point?"

"That's the sort of question we'll never know the answer to," Euphrankes said. "The important thing is, we are here. That couldn't have happened without your help and support. And your design for the portable airlock has proven nothing short of inspired. My estimate is that it has doubled the speed of the road repairs."

"I'm glad to have finally provided some of the service my position was designed to bring to the people," Cumby said. "Now get up there, be careful, and may The Protectors guide you through your journey."

"May they keep you safe until we return," Euphrankes replied.

The two parted, and Euphrankes climbed up after the others. He felt oddly moved by Cumby's words. Not for the first time, he wished his father were alive to see what the things he'd set in motion had come to.

Unlike the crowd on the ground, those grouped atop the platform moved quickly and efficiently about the last minute preparations for takeoff. The last of their supplies were quickly raised up through the new, larger airlocks and stowed in the cargo holds of the *Tangent*.

Aria was waiting when Euphrankes stepped off the ladder. He hugged her quickly and grinned.

"It's going to happen," he said. "Let's get over to the crew's airlock and get on board. We have some checks to run through and if I don't get on board and started doing something soon, I'm likely to explode from the stress."

"I know," she said. "I've had about all the good will and support I can stand."

They slipped away as quickly and quietly as they could, entered the airlock, and made the final ascent to the *Tangent*. Below, a small cheer went up among the workers, which was mirrored by a larger roar from below, but neither of them heard it as the pressurized locks closed tightly behind them.

~ * ~

The bridge was quiet, but busy. The crew was in and out, checking settings, running maintenance procedures and recording the results, and testing everything in sight. They were always careful when launching one of the airships, but this day things had been pushed to a new level. They would only get one shot at survival, and everyone on board felt the tension of the moment. Each had responsibilities, and each was determined that if there were to be a failure, or something overlooked, it would not be on their watch.

Euphrankes smiled and stayed out of their way. He spent his time arranging things to his liking around the chair he would spend his foreseeable future in. He liked to have things just so, and he had gone to great pains to design the captain's chair to his specifications. Now he knew he was just puttering. Everything was organized and neat, exactly as he'd planned it. He just had to have something to fill the next twenty minutes. He knew that once the lifted off, he'd have plenty to occupy his thoughts, but he had to remain sane long enough to let it happen.

"I wish we could slip off to our quarters," Aria said, grinning at him mischievously. "It would make quite the tale for future generations if the Captain and First Officer of the *Tangent* launched into space for the first time from their bed."

"Very funny," Euphrankes said. He tried not to smile, failed, and broke into a huge grin. "It's not as bad an idea as it seems. I believe if I have to just stand here until we launch, I'll go crazy. Have you seen Zins?"

"He's arranging the charts," she said. "He should be up here soon."

Aria nodded to a slanted table in one corner with a glistening brass light fixture mounted to shine directly onto its surface.

"He wants to get the first chart in place and be ready, even though we won't have anything to record until we pass the veil. I think he's as bad off as you and just won't admit it. He's making busy work so he'll have something to do with his brain and his hands."

"Slyphie won't have any such problems," Euphrankes said. "Engineering will be checking and re-checking until lift-off, and then they'll have a fully-manned watch to monitor it all."

"The hard part is going to be getting the second shift to rest before it's their turn," Aria said. "I doubt anyone will be getting much sleep for a while."

"Can't say as I blame them," Euphrankes said. "We'll be seeing things that no one from our planet has ever seen; and we'll be putting ourselves in possible danger we can't even comprehend yet. Who's going to sleep through that?"

"Let's take a quick tour back through engineering, and then get back here for the launch," Aria said. "If you stand there and start worrying over dangers and emergencies we haven't even encountered yet, you'll make me crazy too."

"Good idea," Euphrankes said. "We'll just be sure we keep out of the way. The last thing I want to do is cause more delay."

They left the bridge and entered the chamber that would serve as both galley and ready room during their voyage. In the past, the ready room had been a smaller, separate place where those in command of the ship could meet in private. Euphrankes had felt that this was a very different situation, and he wanted no such obvious division. If they needed to discuss something in private, they had the bridge. Since everyone on board the *Tangent* would be at the same risk if there were problems, then everyone would be welcome at the meetings where they worked to solve them.

The room was centered by a long, sleek table. The seats were gleaming brass, upholstered with soft synthetics. The cushions were Aria's design, tiny Imperium membranes filled with minute amounts of Freethion. They molded comfortably to the body and allowed one to sit for long periods without too much wear and tear on their body. Seeing them made Euphrankes smile. It was exactly the kind of brilliance he'd come to love in his companion and first officer. He himself would have grumbled and groaned through hard metal chairs for the rest of his life, not seeing the obvious solution she'd come up with after only a short bit of thought. She was good at seeing ways to increase the comfort of those around her.

The walls were lined with cabinets that had been carefully secured. Nothing was out of place. The air in between the veils was relatively calm, but they had no idea what they might expect once they got out beyond, and loose equipment flying around was not an option.

Off the main galley were a small kitchen and a sonic cleaning station for dishes. All of their waste would be recycled, cleansed, and reconstituted. They could afford to lose nothing. There was no way to know when they might be able to replenish their supplies. Every system was essential, and every element of their lives had to be monitored carefully, analyzed, and turned back in on itself in as useful a manner as possible.

Beyond the galley, two separate hallways stretched back, and stairs led both up and down to other floors. Along these halls were the crew's quarters, the small library, and a lounge. Euphrankes and Aria's quarters were just behind the bridge to one side, and Zins was berthed across from them, on the far side, in a slightly smaller cabin.

Euphrankes and Aria passed down below those levels

and entered the main engineering chamber. The walls were lined with gauges, valves, pipes and tanks. There were long, slender tanks of Freethion lining the upper and lower sides . . . workbenches and cabinets had been fashioned over and around them. The center of each bulkhead, above the benches, was taken up by the coils and condensers that ran the mag drives. It had all been packed in so carefully that it looked like a mass of shiny metal worms.

There were benches running along the control panels. They allowed one or several engineers to sit at any of the equipment panels at a given time. There were four watch stations set up in the corners of the room, fore and aft, and four engineers were already in place, wearing their protective gear, only the helmets pulled back. It had been agreed that for the passing of the veil, and for several hours afterward, all crew members would be in full gear. They had not tested their ship in space. No one doubted that it would hold—or if they had doubts, they kept them quiet—but there was no reason to take chances straight off the dock.

Euphrankes nodded at the watch standers as they passed, but didn't interrupt. They were doing as he had done on the bridge, arranging things to their liking and familiarizing themselves with a new environment. Anything he said would be nothing more than an unwanted, unnecessary distraction.

They found Slyphie in the workshop/engineering office at the rear of the main compartment. It was outfitted with soldering stations, gauges and test equipment, and lined with cases, boxes, cabinets and tool cases. No space was wasted, and when they found her, Slyphie was doing a final inventory.

"Hey, Skipper," she said as they entered. "Long way from the bridge . . . sure you won't get a nosebleed?"

Euphrankes laughed. He started to tell her not to call him Skipper, and then let it go. Her eyes were bright with energy, and he saw she was as anxious as he was—possibly even more so—to see the ship underway.

"Just taking a last look at everything," he said. "We'll be locked away on that bridge for the foreseeable future. Everything seems under control."

"We've got it covered down here," Slyphie said. "Bonymede is running a last check on the membrane and testing the mag drive. Once we shift from the planetary magnets, we need to be sure we can anchor using the drives, or we'll shoot out through that veil like a rocket."

"I saw the test data and the simulations," Euphrankes said. "We'll be fine."

He looked around the workshop once, nodded, and then pulled the brass watch from his pocket and glanced at the time.

"Well," he said. "This is it. Fifteen minutes from now, we'll be flying . . ."

"Destination destiny," Slyphie said. She snapped a quick salute. "See you on the other side."

Euphrankes took her hand and pulled her close into a quick brotherly hug. Aria hugged her too, and then the two of them hurried back through engineering and up to the bridge. They had to get into their own protective gear, and it would be bad form to be late for the most important moment of their lives.

CHAPTER TWENTY-FOUR

HIGH COUNCILOR CUMBY LEFT THE area of the air tower the moment Euphrankes mounted the steps. He would have liked to be there at ground zero when the great ship launched, but even more he wanted to be in the Chamber of Stars when the *Tangent* burst through the veil. He didn't get around as well as he once had, and the walk to The Temple was a fairly long one.

The streets were empty again—as they had always been, though this time the people were out and together, working toward a common goal. For too many years they'd been locked away in homes, buildings, small factories, and their minds. Everything was suddenly open to them, and it was difficult to rei n in their enthusiasm.

When he reached the door to The Temple, Cyril was waiting for him. Several other priests accompanied the old man, and, again Cumby was struck by the level of energy that surrounded them. The Temple had always been a grim, sedate place. Now things had shifted, and, in combination with the engineers and technicians of the city, Cyril's priests were a vital hub of information, their dusty libraries and dull rituals given new life and purpose.

Many of the older priests had resisted the changes at first, but as their younger counterparts turned to them, calling on their experience, and the knowledge they'd gained through years of service, attitudes had shifted. No one could deny the change in atmosphere, or that it was for the better. The music played in The Temple had energy and enthusiasm behind it. The time standing watch in The Chamber of Stars had become a coveted role rather than something to be avoided, or shunted off to whoever you could convince to take an extra shift.

The library was in The Chamber of Stars, and suddenly the musty tomes and forgotten manuals on those shelves were seen as valuable resources. It seemed as if everyone wanted to find something there that could change things—some lost ritual, or forgotten bit of history that put everything they did, and believed, into new perspective.

In short, the priests had resumed the role that should have been theirs all along. They held the history and the tradition of the city in their care, and they did what they could to improve the mental and spiritual states of the citizens of Urv, who suddenly found themselves with a lot of questions, and the need for direction in a world very different from that in which they'd recently inhabited.

They greeted Cumby's arrival with smiles and nods. Cyril embraced him quickly, and then turned, leading the way to the long stairs that would take them to The Chamber of Stars. Cumby wasn't looking forward to making that climb, but for this he'd have endured much worse.

"This feels a bit different than the last time we all made this climb," Cyril said with a laugh. "A little less frantic, though no less momentous, I think."

"If nothing else," Cumby replied, "it feels more positive. That was a dark day . . ."

"It led to light, and that is the way of darkness," Cyril said. Then he laughed again. "I sound like a passage from one of the old prayers."

"As is only fitting," Cumby said. He kept his words to a minimum as they climbed, saving his breath.

Sensing the effort it was costing the High Councilor, Cyril filled the silence as they progressed, relieving Cumby of the necessity of replies.

"We've made some changes in our watch standing in The Chamber of Stars," he said. Many of our acolytes have asked to be paired with older priests for a time. It seems that over the years the library has become nothing more than a symbolic knowledge store. Upon closer examination, it seems a great deal of things could have been clear to us at a much earlier point in time if we'd just seen what was right there in front of our faces.

"For instance," Cyril went on, "there are copies of the manuals that were kept in the 'forbidden locker' for so long right there in the chamber. Alongside them we found journals filled with the notes of priests who studied there long ago. Many of them had some relatively brilliant ideas.

"We also discovered at least one priest who, through his haste and lack of attention to ritual, nearly brought the pumps to a halt about eighty years ago. It was his actions that caused the creation of the forbidden locker. There were also rules laid out after his banishment. Those rules have kept us rather stagnant for a very long time, and if Euphrankes and young Ozymandes had not taken a chance . . . we might be stagnant still, if not dead."

"What happened?" Cumby asked.

They were nearly to the top of the stairs, and he felt a little better than he'd expected to.

"The priest—his name was Cesaran, believed that he'd found a way to increase the output of the pumps. He brought his findings before The Council, and they urged caution. They suggested, in fact, that The Temple undertake the building of a new pump—one upon which new designs and changes could be tested without putting Urv in danger. Cesaran thought this was foolishly over-cautious. He was very sure of himself, so the next time he was on duty in the pump rooms, he attempted to make his modification to the final pump in the line. His reasoning was that, if he caused a problem, the others would handle the load until he undid his work and returned the last pump to operation.

"As it turned out, his design did, in fact, increase the possible output from the pumps by a considerable amount. What he failed to take into consideration, and what would have been obvious had they tested it as The Council asked, was that the system was designed to handle a certain amount of flow. He modified the pump, put it online, and almost immediately it caused a feedback loop as backed up air was unable to exit the system and turned back on itself, looking for any path of escape."

They'd reached the top of the stairs, and one of the younger priests, who'd hurried on ahead, held the door as first Cyril, and then High Councilor Cumby, entered the room.

"Obviously he didn't destroy the pumps," Cumby said drily. "What happened?"

"He was lucky," Cyril said. "Two others happened to enter the pump room just after the problem ensued. One was older, and wiser than Cesaran. He knew about the valves that Euphrankes discovered, and more. He knew where there was a safety vent. They managed to shunt the system around the final pump, close it down, and release the extra pressure before any real damage was done. They restored the pump to its original state, and, despite his protestations that his work was sound, he was brought before The Council and banished. He was removed from The Temple and sent to farm in one of the agricultural pods."

"They kept his work, though," Cumby said.

"Yes, but they never acted on it. The High Priest at the time worried that his position would lead people to place the blame for such a disaster on his shoulders. Rather than accepting that responsibility as a natural function of the office, he determined to crack down on research and modification. He ordered the locking away of the manuals in the pump room, and I suspect that if he'd known there were other copies in the library, he'd have had them locked away as well. In fact, I get the impression that he was not a very involved High Priest. I think Cesaran's fellows brought the journal up here, and the manuals, and hid them in the hope they would be discovered and studied again, once the trouble had passed."

"So few years to change the entire face of a city," Cumby said. "I can't remember a time when the rituals were not rigid and locked down, and I am an old man, yet from what you say, it must have been only a few years before my birth that these things took place. My parents never spoke of them."

"They would likely not have known," Cyril said. "Unless one of them was a part of The Council, or had some particular affiliation with The Temple, all they'd have known was that the rules had grown harsher, and that it was believed that The Protectors were behind the change. No one ever questioned such edicts, as you know. We dropped into an age of darkness and never even noticed when it happened."

"It's almost time, your eminence," one of the priests called out.

The young man stood beside the telescope. He leaned in again, made some quick adjustments to the lens to focus, and pulled back reluctantly. Every one of them wished to be the one with his eye to that lens when the *Tangent* broke through. They would not voice this out loud, of course.

"I suspect," Cumby said ruefully, "that one of the first orders of business when we are done here will be the commissioning of another telescope or two. Perhaps we should direct them toward different areas of the sky and allow more than one person access. I think that anything we learn in such a fashion might be worth passing on to the *Tangent*, once communications become steady."

"That is a wonderful idea," Cyril said. "For now, though, I believe you should take the honors . . ."

Cumby took a step toward the telescope, stopped, and shook his head.

"You are the chosen communicator," he said. "You are the one with the ability and proclivity to record events as they happen. If any should watch this moment, it should be you. You are more likely to be able to share what you see—to bring it to life in the telling, and writing of it. I have a poor imagination, and at this age, a memory to match. I will be content to take a glance after they are free of the veil."

Cyril thought about it for a moment, and then nodded. He stepped forward and gripped the telescope in one hand, taking the seat behind it. He placed one eye against the lens, and no one in the room spoke. It was as if the sound and breath had been sucked from them.

"There she is," Cyril said softly. "The *Tangent* is approaching the veil."

CHAPTER TWENTY-FIVE

THE *TANGENT* SHIFTED JUST SLIGHTLY to the side as it lifted free of the final mooring and drifted up and away from the air tower. Those below quickly shrank to the size of tiny insects, and then faded from sight as Euphrankes steered the great ship in a looping curve away from Urv.

They'd determined that it would be best to be clear of all cities and roads before making their shot at the veil, but at the same time they wanted to remain within clear sight of Urv's telescope. There was little fear of damaging the veil after what they'd witnessed recently, but as Cumby had pointed out to Euphrankes over tea—they had never shot anything out of the veil. They had only witnessed something flying in. They also didn't really know what damage that passing might have caused to the falling debris. It could have been much larger before passing through the veil, reduced by friction or some other force they were unaware of.

It had been suggested that they try and launch a projectile through first, but the idea had been rejected. It might cause unnecessary wear or damage to the veil, and other than actually seeing it pass through the veil, there was no way to judge what effect this would have, unless they allowed it to plunge back to the planet. If they did this outside the First Veil, they had no way to study or retrieve it, and if it struck the veil they'd have a new disaster on their hands that might not turn out like the first.

Now, as they rose in a slow, spiraling loop, picking up speed with each narrowing circle, Euphrankes wondered if they'd been rash. He believed that The Second Veil functioned on a molecular level. It was not, as the First Veil, a solid shield against objects or attack. Its purpose was to prevent particular types of gas from being lost from the atmosphere. It was a giant, radiant bubble that prevented the thin upper air from dispersing into space, and provided a temperature and atmospheric buffer between empty space, and the First Veil.

It was also possible that Euphrankes was wrong. He tried to set those thoughts aside and concentrate. The ship steered like a dream. They'd determined that, rather than just go nose to the sky and blast up, it would be better to give the ship a sort of second shake-down as they rose, taking the circular route, and then, just before contacting the veil, raising the ship's nose, reversing polarity on the mag drives holding them close to the planet and shooting up the last few miles directly into space.

"Just past the halfway point, Frankes," Zins called out.

They were all strapped carefully into their seats. When the drives reversed, the force pressing them down would be immense. If anyone were standing, or not tied in firmly, they might be slammed into a bulkhead hard enough to kill them. Their protective suits were fully sealed. The face shields were made of synthetic glass. Tiny spun threads of Imperium ran through the material, giving it a slight flexibility, and strengthening it nearly a thousand times. The shields were designed to withstand a sudden change of pressure, and the synth-glass, very similar to that which provided their view of the endless sky above them, glistened with subtle hints of the embedded filaments.

"Going to keep her steady a bit longer," Euphrankes said. "Aria, can you get a report from engineering?"

Aria nodded. She flipped a switch and spoke into an ornate microphone mounted beside her seat. The communications system was of her own design, and every time he saw it, Euphrankes had to smile. Aria never went for simple and utilitarian if flashy and elegant was a choice.

The microphone stood on a tripod and was adjustable so that she could sit at any of the various control panels available to her and use it comfortably. A series of toggle switches determined which circuit she was plugged into. She could reach any department or space, flip it over to the long-range communicator on line with The Temple, or turn the microphones toward space, open up a wide-band receiver, and search for unexpected or unknown signals. Euphrankes would have gone with a headset that plugged into one of the panels, but he'd left it to her—and found that he approved.

The *Tangent* wasn't just another airship. She was the first of her kind—an interstellar cruiser. The bridge should be elegant—extravagant, even.

"Engineering," Aria spoke clearly and crisply, "report."

The answer was clear and immediate, and after another quick adjustment it emanated from speakers all over the bridge.

"Smooth and steady," Slyphie said. "Not a shiver or a glitch."

"Perfect," Euphrankes said. "Get a report from all stations. Make sure the entire crew is strapped in and ready. We will be reversing the drive in five minutes."

Aria flipped another switch, and red lights began flashing around the bridge. A soft, throbbing buzz sounded—not jarring, but loud enough to carry. Euphrankes knew it was the same all over the ship. It was the warning to get seated and strapped. He also knew that everyone had been strapped in for the last twenty minutes. It was procedure, and he thought it was best to begin their first flight safely.

He wished for a moment that he'd prepared a speech, but then thought better of it. The Second Veil was approaching quickly. Beyond it, vast screen of darkness, lit only by twinkling stars and the pale surfaces of the twin moons. None of the crew would want him to mar the memory by speaking. Each of them would share this moment, one with the other, but they would do it in the solitude of their thoughts, minds, and dreams.

"Three minutes," he said softly.

He tightened the spiral slightly, edging the nose upward. He glanced at the face of the timer in front of him, mesmerized, as the hand moved slowly from number to number.

"One minute," he said.

He straightened the nose of the *Tangent* and it hung there, seeming to float free in the sky for just an instant. There was a hum as the mag drives spun. The acceleration, just from the unbound Freethion, was huge. They were pressed back slowly into their seats as the *Tangent* shot forward. Then the drives kicked in and—as if they'd been fired from a gun—they shot into space. It happened so quickly that by the time they caught their breath, they were through and speeding away from the planet. Behind them, the tear in the veil sealed as if it had never happened, glistening like a shimmering spray of water, sending rainbow glitters of light trailing after them as they soared into the void.

CHAPTER TWENTY-SIX

IN THE CHAMBER OF STARS, Cyril gasped. His fingers tightened around the telescope, and he leaned even closer.

"What?" High Councilor Cumby cried, unable to contain himself. "What do you see? What happened?"

"They . . . are free," Cyril said. He leaned back and stood, stepping away from the telescope. Cumby slide into the seat and pressed his eye to the lens. At first he saw nothing but the stars, the veil, and the twin moons. Then, as his vision acclimated, he could make out a smaller shape, glistening like a chip of silver, moving slowly across the darkness.

"Can you contact them?" Cumby asked. "The radio, is it live?"

Cyril glanced across the room to a priest who'd been standing by, waiting for instructions. He had the microphone in his hand. The speaker, a large, cone-shaped device, was aimed toward the center of the room so anyone present would be able to hear it.

The man turned to the radio, but before he could key the microphone, a burst of static crackled from the speaker. It was followed by a second burst, a quick, frequency shifting squeal . . . and then Aria's voice.

"Chamber of Stars this is *Tangent*. We have achieved space. I repeat. We have achieved space. Can you read us?"

The priest stood very still, staring at the speaker, the microphone forgotten in his hand. Cyril waited only a second before hurrying across the room and gently pulling it from the younger man's grasp.

He keyed the microphone and spoke.

"*Tangent*, this is Chamber of Stars. We read you very clearly. Congratulations, and we are thankful you are safe."

They waited a moment, and then Aria replied. "As are we, Cyril . . . as are we. All systems are operating as expected, except we have not yet been able to lock the mag drive onto another source of metal. Our velocity is not decreasing; as expected, there is no resistance beyond the veil."

Cyril glanced over at Cumby and smiled. Then he shrugged.

"*Tangent*," he said. "I had planned all sorts of important messages. I had so many questions scant moments ago. Now—instead—I will share with you a single moment in my life. It may prove to be the most miraculous thing I have ever witnessed.

"Moments ago, through the telescope, I saw you approaching The Second Veil. You seemed to be floating, moving very slowly. Then, in an instant—so quickly that, had I blinked at the wrong moment, I would have missed it, you shot into the void. The Veil shimmered. From the point where you impacted it, light rippled outward, alive with color. When you were through, it snapped tight, as if you had torn through a bubble that refused to pop. Where it sealed, there was an opaque circle, just for a second. Then it was as if nothing had passed, and I saw you on the other side. High Councilor Cumby is watching you now. I would tell you to wave, but you are nothing but a glimmer."

"Thank you for sharing that," Aria replied. "I am handing

over communications to Euphrankes, who would like to offer something in trade."

A moment passed, there was another static crackle, and then Euphrankes voice, as clear as if he'd stood beside them, flowed from the speaker.

"From where I sit," he said, "I have a view behind us via Bonymede's miraculous mirrors and lenses. What I see is very, very beautiful. The planet, from here, is a globe. The veil shimmers all around it with every color imaginable. Beneath that, the roads, and the cities glow. It's like an intricate drawing made with light. You can make out little in detail, but the whole is a sight I will never forget. If I can, I will find a crewmember with the skill to draw it in the log."

"I suspect," Cyril replied, "that you will bring a great many wonders. I look forward to the day we can go through that log together."

There was a moment of silence, and then Euphrankes voice came across again.

"We have a lock," he said. "We are testing the mag drives, and all seems to be working even more smoothly than expected. There is literally no resistance out here. I'm going to have to do some calculations to understand the full implications. It may mean several other systems won't work at all."

Cyril laughed.

"If anyone is equipped to meet such a challenge, it is you, Euphrankes Holymnn. Travel with The Protectors watching over your shoulder. And before you are completely out of sight, ask your Navigator to show you the final gift we've given you."

There as another moment of silence, and the Euphrankes chuckled. "It's perfect. Thank you, my friend. I will gaze upon it often. When we return, maybe we'll know what it means.

"For now, we are signing off. I need to run a systems check, and to be certain everyone in the crew made it as safely as we did here on the bridge. We will be in contact in a few hours at the appointed time. *Tangent*, signing off."

"Chamber of Stars, offline," Cyril said softly. He glanced down and chuckled as he realized he'd forgotten to key the microphone.

"They really did it," Cumby said. He stood and let the other priests, one by one, have a look at the dwindling sliver of the great ship receding from sight. "By The Protectors, Cyril, they actually did it."

"That they did," Cyril agreed. "What remains to be seen is—what will it lead to."

"The future," Cumby said, turning toward the door. "According to a great man I know—it's a place worth visiting."

On the bridge of the *Tangent*, Euphrankes unstrapped himself and stood. He walked over to the chart table where Maester Zins sat with a big grin on his face. On the table, standing upright on a small metal stand, was the shard of debris with the unknown message on it.

"What do you mean?" Euphrankes asked it softly. "And where did you come from?"

He turned, and he stared off into space, the letters *Lockhe d* strobed before his eyes.

"Mag drive is at full power," Aria reported.

Euphrankes returned to his seat, strapped in and gripped the arms tightly.

"Then, by all means," he said. "Take us out of here."

The ship shivered just slightly, and then, with a rush of force that pressed them into their seats once again, shot out toward the stars. Behind them their planet, their world, and their past dwindled to a small dot of reflected light . . . and winked out. As their speed leveled off, the pressure decreased, and Euphrankes was able to smile again. It was a very long time before he stopped.

Acknowledgments

First, and foremost, as always, I want to thank my family for putting up with me, the writing, the books and the dreams. Trish, love of my life, Bill, Stephanie, Zach, Zane, and Katie—and even Gizmo the fuzzball, Sid the not so vicious cat, and Pookie the never-to-be-a-coat chinchilla. Love you all.

Second, and importantly, I'd like to thank my cohorts in crime, Steven Savile and Aaron Rosenberg, and all those who will follow after as we build and expand The Scattered Earth saga. It's been fun, and it's working. Two things that so seldom go together. May we retire and die rich in all things that matter; and may we leave our mark—I guess that's what writers have been trying to do since the first rock scratch on a cave wall.

Finally—and not least—I want to thank the inspirational crew of the Airship Axis—Frank Holman (Euphrankes) Skip Zinsmeister (Maester Zins) Patrick Cumby (High Councilor Cumby) Tery McIntire, (Terrmac)—Jen and Ray who show up momentarily, and all my co-workers who have generously (and often without their knowledge) lent their names to my stories and new worlds. I have one of the greatest jobs on earth—and I don't even mean the writing.

Want to read more
tales of the Scattered Earth?
Turn the page for a sample
from the first book
in another Scattered Earth series:

SCATTERED EARTH
DREAD REMORA

THE BIRTH OF THE DREAD REMORA
AARON ROSENBERG

CHAPTER ONE

MIDSHIPMAN NATHANIEL DEMMING GLANCED AT his pocket watch again, the luminous face easily readable through the water. T minus four to launch. *No worries, old boy,* he told himself. *After all, we're about to attempt the first launch of an untested ship with an untried crew and an uninformed captain, on a mission to an unexplored domain after an unexplained target.*

Why fret?

"T minus four to launch," Lizette Mills reported from the helm. Demming hid a smile. She was half a second off in her count, but what did that matter? And what would he possibly gain by pointing that out now? Far better to keep silent and rib her about it later, in the officers' mess. Lizette was always a fun one to rib.

"Roger that," Captain Mendez replied, sitting tall in the command chair. From his position behind her Demming could still make out the topknot of her dark blond braid beneath her cap. Not a hair out of place, as usual. "Are we secure?"

That last was directed at him, Demming realized after a heartbeat, and scanned his console, studying the readouts. "Secure, captain," he confirmed a few seconds later. His heart was thudding so loudly it was a wonder the water was rippling all around him. "All crew in their harnesses, all ports locked down."

"Good. Mister Dittmer?"

"All secure, Captain," the quartermaster replied right away, his voice as lazy as always. With any other man Demming would have assumed he had taken the time to double-check while the captain was waiting for his answer first, but with Dittmer he knew that wasn't the case. Dittmer didn't need extra time. He already knew where every scrap of material was on this ship. The man had a memory like a clamshell, latched on tight.

"T minus three," Lizette updated. Everyone on the foredeck tensed with anticipation. Behind him Demming heard someone, most likely one of the ensigns, gasp for breath—and start choking as water filled his lungs. Classic rookie mistake. A wave of quiet laughter filled the cabin. Demming could hardly blame the ensign, though. It was all he could do to keep his own mouth closed, nostrils clamped shut, gills narrowed. What he really wanted was to start gasping himself, but that would never do. He was a midshipman of the line, for current's sake! He had not only his own dignity but the dignity of the entire ship and the entire Royal Navy to maintain!

Plus the others would laugh at him just as they were all laughing at the ensign now. And that was no way to begin a mission. Especially this mission.

"T minus two."

"Throttle us up, Miss Mills," Mendez ordered. Lizette nodded, her hand going to the smooth coral inlay of the throttle and easing it down a quarter toward the console. Beneath and all around him Demming could feel the thrum as the ship's engines started to spin.

Soon. Very soon.

"T minus one."

"Ready on my mark," the captain warned. She reached for the speaking tube built into the arm of her chair, and her next words echoed faintly, as they repeated from speakers all throughout the ship. "Ladies and gentlemen, we are about to embark on our mission. I consider it an honor and a privilege to lead you into history. May the waves grant us success, and water save the queen."

"Water save the queen," Demming repeated softly, along with the other officers and, no doubt, the seamen in their compartments. And water save us, he thought. But did not say out loud.

"Mark!" Mendez hissed, and Lizette's quick fingers tapped controls, releasing the clamps that bound them to the docks and slamming the throttle down full. With a roar and a twist the ship's engines boomed to life, revving instantly to full speed, and with a mighty rushing sound the *HMES Remora* shot up from the ocean floor, her long, tapered prow pointed up at the air and at the stars beyond.

The force of their acceleration slammed Demming back in his seat, and he was grateful for the webbing that secured him there. He gripped the armrests on either side, feet planted flat on the floor, and kept his eyes squarely on the narrow windows that sliced down over the foredeck and arced along it toward its nose. For now all he could see was water, lit by the *Remora*'s powerful searchlights but shifting past too quickly to leave any real impression. This was the easy part, however. He had seen all of this before.

It was what came next that would be a shock.

In what seemed only moments but Demming knew had to be closer to an hour the water began to lighten. He could make out fish and reefs rushing by. They were nearing the surface. He felt his lungs constrict at the very thought of it.

The surface!

"Prepare for wave breach!" Lizette announced, her hand tightening on the throttle to one side and her fingers poised over the sonic pulse array to the other.

"All hands, hold fast!" Captain Mendez ordered through the speakers.

The water continued to brighten, forcing Demming to squint against the glare. He fought the instinct to turn away, or close his eyes. He had to watch this. After all, how many could say they had experienced true wave breach? And he wanted to remember all of this journey, every second, so that he could chronicle it later. For posterity.

Or for those who wondered what became of them.

With a surge of sound that set the hull ringing, the *Remora*'s prow burst upward through the waves. The light was blinding. Demming blinked, trying to clear his sight, and after a few seconds he found he could see again. It was so bright! And so empty!

His body pushed back in his chair, feeling heavy and sluggish. The *Remora* groaned around them. The noise had increased when they'd broken through, but the sense of momentum had dimmed rapidly. Now it felt as if they were barely moving, yet he could make out strange white shapes, filmy like jellyfish but puffed out like ink clouds, appearing in view and then vanishing below. So they must still be rising.

But for how long? Even now the waters exerted their hold, attempting to draw the ship back into the deeps.

"Sonic pulse on my mark!" Captain Mendez told Lizette. She didn't shout—their two chairs were less than a body-length apart—but every word was crisp and clear.

"Aye aye, captain!" Lizette tensed at the ready.

"Mark!"

The pilot's fingers jabbed down on the array, and the *Remora* shuddered as a rush of energy exploded behind her. Demming held his breath. All of this had worked in theory, and on the probe, but they had never had the chance to test it on a real ship, with a real crew.

This was the test.

Right now.

With them in it.

He waited, not sure what he was expecting. But after a second he realized that the *Remora* was still rising. If anything, her velocity had increased. It had worked!

"Again!" Mendez ordered, and Lizette complied. The ship shook again, though some of that faded as Lizette throttled down the impellers to three-quarter speed, and the *Remora* leaped skyward again, forced upward by the focused sonic burst it had just released behind.

And above—

Demming peered through the window. The sky was lighter and lighter in color as they rose, approaching pure white now, and through it he could just make out the twinkling of lights.

The stars.

They were close.

"How soon?" Mendez demanded. The question didn't seem aimed at anyone in particular, so it was her first lieutenant, Daniel Holst, who answered.

"Fifty kilometers and closing, captain," he reported. "And all systems are performing admirably."

"Thank you, Mister Holst." Demming could hear the smile

in her voice. "Miss Mills, please continue."

"Yes, captain." Lizette fired off another sonic pulse, the energy wave pushing off the waves and earth below and propelling the *Remora* further. The pressure was immense, slamming everyone into their seats, causing whines and creaks from spots along the hull and around the inner port, making it hard to breathe, hard to focus, hard to think. Demming kept his eyes trained on the stars beyond and took short, shallow breaths, letting the water filter into his gills almost of its own accord. The scientists had all agreed this pressure would let up once they breached the air. And they were so close! Almost— almost—

Wham!

The *Remora* lurched as if she had slammed into a strong current head-on. The ship flipped onto its side, all its momentum spent, listing and drifting with the dregs of that lost velocity. Water buffeted Demming, slapping his face and hands and chest and legs, and again he resisted the impulse to gulp for breath. Beyond the window, the glare had suddenly winked out, replaced by a darkness as deep as any abyss. There had been no lights in the cabin—none had seemed necessary—and in the sudden darkness only the telltales on various consoles could be seen. And here and there the gleam of those lights reflected in wide, terrified eyes.

And there was silence.

Demming had found the noise deafening as they'd shot through the air, but its absence was far worse. He had expected normal sounds, if slightly diminished—the roll of the waves, the rush of water through the impellers, the hum of the engines, the song of whales and chatter of dolphins and flutter of fish.

Here? Here there was nothing.

Everyone, it seemed, was holding their collective breath.

And then the sounds came all at once. But only from within the *Remora* herself.

Shouting. Whispering. Cursing. Whimpering. Even crying.

The ship generated its own wave of noise as crew and officers alike began to panic.

Demming fought down his own urge to do likewise. This would not do! This was a ship of the line! They had their honor to maintain!

He forced himself to calm down, to breathe slowly and evenly. He unclenched his hands where they had dug into the armrests. He uncurled his toes and set his feet flat against the floor once more. And he waited.

Waited for the captain to tell them what to do.

Captain Mendez was an experienced captain. Not of a ship like this, of course—no one was. But she had years of training handling other vessels, and crews this size and even larger. She was quiet and competent and very much by-the-books. He knew that, once she had taken time to collect herself, she would regain control and restore order.

So Demming waited.

The seconds seemed to stretch on. The cacophony did not diminish. If anything, it grew in volume and diversity as more of his shipmates found their voice. There was thrashing as many wrestled with their harnesses, and banging throughout the Remora indicated that at least some had already worked their way free, though to what end Demming could not imagine.

He was content to sit and await orders.

Until he heard the one thing he had feared the most.

It began as a whisper. Rapidly it grew into a wail, a single ululation that soon spread into words.

Words that chilled him to the very soul.

"Oh, great wave!" were the words that struck terror into his heart and blood. "Great wave, we're lost! We've been consumed by the abyss! Our souls will be devoured by the darkness!"

All other sounds on the foredeck ceased, then, as every officer turned to stare at the command chair—and their tall, blond captain, who curled up in it, sobbing and crying out in despair.

Looking to try a new series?
Perhaps something a little bit supernatural,
a little bit alien . . . a little bit O.C.L.T.
Turn the page for a sneak peek
at the first book
in the new O.C.L.T. series:

Chapter One

IN A LOW BUNKER IN the desert near the border of Jordan and the Dead Sea, a dozen men had gathered. They arrived over a period of hours, none too close to the other to avoid being seen together. They were not men given to solitary excursions, but each had left comrades and guards behind in the interest of security. They were robed, and their faces were covered against the whipping desert sand. Far above, the moon shone pale and cloaked in clouds.

Salt clusters along the bank of the water glimmered oddly, almost glowing in the dim light. The water was as flat and lifeless as a sheet of glass. None of the twelve even glanced at it, though the last of them stopped and gazed directly across the surface toward Jerusalem. He stood there for only a moment, and then passed between the two squat, expressionless guards stationed outside the door. The two were associated with none of the twelve. They were carefully vetted mercenaries without affiliation. They did not know who they guarded, or why, and they didn't care, as long as they were paid well, and on time.

Inside the building was a single long room. There was a small kitchenette, and a bathroom, but these were sealed. The room was centered by a long rectangular table set very low to the ground. The twelve gathered around it. There were drinks, but for the most part they were ignored. The room was lit by a single lamp on the table, as if those present weren't even comfortable knowing one another, let alone getting a good look.

When they were all seated, the man at the head of the table leaned back, glanced around at the others, and shook his head.

"We represent," he began, "an incredible gathering of power. The resources we command should be able to move mountains –with or without faith. We can, and have, bought kings and ambassadors."

"And for all of that," one of those to his left growled, "we have failed once again at the one task we must accomplish before all others."

There were mumbles of agreement all around. None of those gathered were happy, and each secretly blamed the others for their failure. They were not men accustomed to failure, or the denial of their desires. They dealt in blood, fortunes, and power. The one thing they shared—the one central binding power—was the passion of their faith. They were from a variety of nationalities, but theirs was a common enemy and a holy cause.

"Sometimes," the man who'd first spoken continued, "I feel as if we have lost our way. Allah places more obstacles in our way than he removes, and despite our unwavering loyalty, the Holy City is yet in the hands of the unclean. They have proclaimed themselves God's People to the world. What have we been proclaimed?"

"Killers," one of the others said.

"Terrorists," a third cut in. "They say that we care about nothing but the shedding of innocent blood. No matter that our beliefs are those of our fathers, and our father's fathers. No

The Parting

matter that the blasphemy of our most Holy City being handed by Western dogs to the unclean cuts us to the very soul."

He slammed his fist on the table. As sturdy as it was, the glasses and lamp jumped. Still, none of them rose. Their passion simmered, but it did not boil over. Nothing that had been said was new. Theirs was an old hatred, and it burned slowly, but with great heat. It was fueled by frustration and the futility of their efforts.

"There must be a way," the first man spoke again. "Allah will show us that way."

The grim semi-silence of the gathering was broken by a peal of rich, feminine laughter. They spun as a single unit, drawing blades, and guns and diving back from the table with cries of surprise. They were leaders, but each of them had earned their position through years in the field. None of them was privileged by birth, and if they'd been compromised, every man of them would fight to the death.

There was no invading force. There was only a lone woman, covered from head to toe in traditional Arab robes. Her head was swathed in a dark hijab, covering all but her face. It was a remarkable face. Despite the dim light, her eyes glittered, and the grim line of her mouth was bent in a scornful frown. She stood with her arms crossed in front of her, glaring down at them as if she belonged –as if her presence did not break every law of their faith. As if all their security was so much dust in the desert.

"So," she said at last. "You have come to wallow in your defeat. How clever of you. How proud you must be. Allah would be pleased."

The first of the men back to his feet closed on her, his dagger raised.

The woman cocked her head and watched him, making no move to retreat.

"Who are you?" he asked. "How do you come here?"

"I came on the wind," she replied. "I come because you have called me. I come—because you have failed."

"You will not leave this place alive," the man said.

"I will," she said. "I will leave as I came, and I will leave with your promise, and your aid. You may call me Amunet."

The man closed on her quickly. He was not in the mood for idle chatter. He drove the dagger straight at her heart, but she only smiled. She spoke a single word—a word none of them heard clearly, and that none of them would have understood had they heard it.

The dagger shimmered and lost its rigidity. It turned back on itself, writhed and squirmed in the man's grip. He screamed, and tried to release it, but—now a serpent—it had coiled around his wrist and moved up his arm toward his face. It was fast, and he staggered back, crashed into the table and fell across it

Two of the others ran to his side. One gripped the serpent behind its head, and the other dragged it free of his wrist. They held it—and then—with a cry of his own, the man gripping the neck cried out and backed away. His hand dripped blood, and he stared in shock.

The dagger fell to the floor between them. The twelve turned and stared. Amunet gazed back at them, unperturbed.

"You will listen to me," she said. "You will help me, and I will help you. Though I am certain that my words are wasted, I will tell you this—there is nothing you can do to prevent it."

"Sorceress!" one of the men cried. "Allah protect us!"

Despite what they'd just witnessed, these were hard men.

The Parting

They were not going to be taken down by a simple illusion, and they were unused to being spoken to as lackeys—or for that matter, by women whom they had not addressed first. The frustration of their recent endeavors, coupled with the ignominy of the situation was too much. They spread out and moved in quickly. They did not speak, they acted, but the woman, Amunet, did not back away. She raised both of her hands and spoke in clear, cutting tones.

Again, her words were lost to them. She seemed to speak in tongues, though now and then a phrase made the ghost of sense. The already dim light darkened, and there was a rising wail from outside the building. They ignored it. Before any of them could reach where the woman stood, the wailing was joined by twin screams.

They hesitated and turned toward the single door. There were no further screams, but the wail had grown to a roar, as if the desert had lifted up to sweep them away.

"What is it?" one of them cried. "What is happening?"

"Sandstorm!" another yelled. "It must be a storm. What else could…"

The door slammed inward as if struck by a huge hammer. It crashed open and hit the wall so hard the stout wood cracked. A dark cloud roared through and spread like smoke. The wail they'd heard was now a droning, pulsing wall of sound. Before they could even back away, the swarm of locusts struck them. They were driven back, pounded into the walls, covered head to foot in biting, buzzing death. They screamed, and as they did, their mouths were filled. They tumbled back, scrambled for cover that did not exist, and through it all, Amunet stood, untouched, unmoving.

When the twelve were down, covered and helpless, crawling

with her plague, she clapped her hands and shouted a single word.

In that second, there was absolute silence. The locusts had vanished. The door swung loose on its hinges. The light flickered once, threatened to go out, and then grew steady once more. Amunet walked to the table and straightened it. The twelve scuttled back against the walls, watching her in terror-stricken awe. She met their gaze, not smiling, not angry. When she saw they would not speak again, she nodded very slightly.

"Now," she said, "you will listen. There is work to be done, and if you hope to know the glory of your vision, you will act swiftly and exactly as I command. You have prayed, and you have maintained your faith. I am here. Your ancestors, long ago, faced off with the Hebrew sorcerer Moses—and their hearts were weak. Mine is strong, and I offer that strength to you. In exchange, you will bring me what I need. The Holy Land will grow strong—you will be great in the eyes of Allah, and of the world. I will have what is mine."

One by one, the men rose from where they'd fallen. They checked themselves for dangers that were not there. One of them walked to the door and, after glancing out to see that the two guards lay dead in the sand, closed it as well as he could. They righted the chairs and returned to their seats. When they were ready, Amunet began to speak, and they listened very carefully. They listened long into the night, and then, when she was finished, they dispersed as randomly and as quietly as they'd arrived.

When she was alone in the room, Amunet finally allowed her lip to curl in a dark, enigmatic smile. She turned out the lamp, and as the light drained from the room—she was gone.

ABOUT THE AUTHOR

DAVID NIALL WILSON HAS BEEN writing and publishing horror, dark fantasy, and science fiction since the mid-eighties. An ordained minister, once President of the Horror Writer's Association and multiple recipient of the Bram Stoker Award, his novels include *Maelstrom*, *The Mote in Andrea's Eye*, *Deep Blue*, the Grails Covenant Trilogy, *Star Trek Voyager: Chrysalis*, *Except You Go Through Shadow*, *This is My Blood*, *Ancient Eyes*, *On the Third Day*, *The Orffyreus Wheel*, and *Vintage Soul*. *Heart of a Dragon*—the chronological first book in the DeChance Chronicles is now available. The Stargate Atlantis novel *Brimstone*, written with Patricia Lee Macomber is his most recent title in print—upcoming are *The Parting*, the first novel in the O. C. L. T. series, and *Maelstrom*, a limited HC from Bad Moon Books. He has over 150 short stories published in anthologies, magazines, and five collections, the most recent of which were "Defining Moments" published in 2007 by WFC Award-winning Sarob Press, and the currently available "Ennui & Other States of Madness," from Dark Regions Press. His work has appeared in and is due out in various anthologies and magazines. David lives and loves with Patricia Lee Macomber in Hertford, NC with their children, Billy, Zach, Zane, and Katie, and occasionally their genius college daughter Stephanie, their ridiculous Pekingese Gizmo, their not-so-vicious cat, Sid, and a never-to-become-a-coat chinchilla named Pookie.

David is CEO and founder of Crossroad Press, a cutting-edge digital publishing company specializing in electronic novels, collections, and non-fiction, as well as unabridged audiobooks. Visit Crossroad Press at http://store.crossroadpress.com.

PRAISE FOR DAVID NIALL WILSON'S WORK:

For *Deep Blue*: "Wilson demonstrates that a horror novel doesn't need gallons of blood to succeed, that spiritual terror can be even more effective." —*Publisher's Weekly*

"This is an exquisite meditation upon the nature of pain and redemption written with a blues sensibility that rolls through the mind like bleak, resounding chords of dark music. The perfect novel for a hot, sultry night." —J. L. Comeau—CountGore.com

For *This is My Blood*: "Wilson's prose is smooth and powerful, carrying its allegorical weight with grace. His first novel is one of the most unique vampire stories to appear in recent years, balancing themes of damnation and prophesy against those of faith and redemption." —*Publisher's Weekly*

For *The Orffyreus Wheel*: "The book started off with a bang. From page one the book is intense and filled with suspense." —Blondie—Amazon.com

Curious about other Crossroad Press books?
Stop by our site:
http://store.crossroadpress.com
We offer quality writing
in digital, audio, and print formats.

Enter the code FIRSTBOOK
to get 20% off your first order from our store!
Stop by today!

www.ingramcontent.com/pod-product-compliance
Lightning Source LLC
Chambersburg PA
CBHW060434180626
46817CB00007B/2804